Dec. 2008

Merry Christmas!
    Adam had his c
but he turned out to be a time
person. I think you will enjoy his
story.
        Love you Hunter.
            Grandma Wilcox

Adam's story

Adam has his ups and downs
but he turned out to be a fine
person. I think you will enjoy his
Grandma Wilcox

Adam's story

A NOVEL BY

JACK WEYLAND

**DESERET
BOOK**

SALT LAKE CITY, UTAH

Library of Congress Cataloging-in-Publication Data

Weyland, Jack, 1940-
Adam's story / Jack Weyland.
    p.   cm.
Sequel to: Charly.
ISBN-10 1-59038-248-X (pbk.)
ISBN-13 978-1-59038-248-6 (pbk.)
    1. Mormon missionaries—Fiction.   2. Grandparent and adult child—Fiction.   3. Mothers—Death—Fiction.   4. Mormon families—Fiction.   5. Stepmothers—Fiction.   6. New Jersey—Fiction.   I. Title.
PS3573.E99 A67 2003
813'.54—dc22   2003019947

Printed in the United States of America
Malloy Lithographing Incorporated, Ann Arbor, MI

10   9   8   7

To our wonderful grandchildren

1

As soon as Elder Norton and I left the commuter train, I looked at the address that I had secretly scribbled on a scrap of paper and stuck in my wallet twenty-one months earlier, just before leaving on my mission.

Except for this unauthorized little excursion, we were on our way back to our apartment after a zone conference.

"Welcome to Madison, New Jersey, Elder," I said to Norton as we hurried down the stairs from the commuter train-stop to ground level. It was the first Wednesday in January, and it had been cold and drizzly all day.

Norton was tall and skinny, and his dark brown hair never got out of place. People trusted him because he spoke softly and took great pains to choose his words carefully. Those were also the qualities that drove me crazy.

"We shouldn't be here," he said, fixing his gaze on the ground. He only made eye contact when there was complete agreement.

"How can you say that?"

"Well, for starters, we're out of our area."

1

"We're *in transit*, Elder," I said.

He thought about it while I looked at a map of the town. "We were in transit on the train," he said, "but now that we've left the train, we're no longer in transit. We're out of our area."

"Think of it as a slight detour to our area," I said. "Let's go."

Reluctantly he kept up with me but continued whining. "This is no detour. We're out of our area, and we're breaking mission rules."

I shrugged. "Well, maybe so, but it's something I've been promising myself I'd do since coming on my mission."

Even though I sounded confident, I did have misgivings. I knew President McNamara wouldn't approve of what we were about to do, but more than that, I knew my mom wouldn't like it. It was also out of character for me to break mission rules. Even when I was growing up, I'd never had any kind of a rebellious streak.

We walked past the fire station and a couple of stately church buildings, and then the street became residential. The bare branches of tall trees formed a web-like canopy over the street.

It began to rain again. After a couple of blocks we turned left down a less-traveled street. A sign said we were headed toward the town library.

"What are we going to say if the elders assigned here catch us in their area?" he asked.

"They're not going to even know we were here. This will just take a minute, and then we'll be on our way again."

"Who are the people we're going to visit?"

"They're part of my family."

"Are they expecting us?"

"Not really."

"How come?"

"I'm not sure how happy they'll be to see me, so I thought we'd just drop in and see how things go." I checked the

2

address written on the scrap of paper. "It's that house. I'll take the door."

Norton checked his watch. "We don't have much time. We have a seven o'clock."

"We'll be okay."

"You knew we were going to come here this morning during companion planning, didn't you? So, why didn't you discuss it with me then?"

The answer was obvious. If I'd told him my plans, he would have told President McNamara at our zone conference.

We walked up the path to the front door. It was a well-kept, two-story, white-frame house, older and more modest than the other houses on the street. Back in my neighborhood in Salt Lake City, it would have been considered an expensive home, but here, with the two houses on either side being in the million dollar price range, it looked almost shabby in contrast.

Norton was still venting. "Why even have companionship planning if you won't talk to me about your plans? We need to talk more."

"We'll talk, Elder, we'll talk."

"You always say that, but we never do."

"We're talking now."

"We need to work together, we need to be a team. Sometimes I feel like you have no respect for me as a person."

Being with Norton was a lot like being in a troubled marriage.

I knocked on the door.

The woman who answered looked like she'd dedicated her life to reversing the aging process. Her hair, which should have been gray, was the color of a new penny. She wore a velvety looking, chocolate brown kind of pant suit thing and big gold loopy earrings.

Once she opened the door and got a look at us, she scowled, "We're not interested."

3

"I'm Adam."

A man's voice called out from inside the house. "Who is it?"

"Jehovah's Witnesses . . . again."

"I'm Adam," I repeated.

"Tell 'em we're not interested!" the man inside hollered. His voice was raspy but carried throughout the house.

"I told 'em that!"

"Tell 'em again. They never take no for an answer the first time."

She turned to face us. "We're really not interested."

"I'm your grandson, Adam. My birthmother's name was Charlene, but everyone called her Charly."

She was in the process of closing the door when what I'd said finally registered. Her mouth dropped open, and she covered it with her hand. "Heaven help us," she said softly.

"You're talking religion with 'em, aren't you?" the man called out. "Look, whatever you do, don't let 'em in! If you do, we'll never get rid of 'em."

She was staring at me like I was a ghost or something. "Please, come in," she said softly.

My first impression on entering their house was that she, like my mom, watched home decorating shows on TV. The windows were draped with layers of fabric, and every couch had five or six little pillows that served no purpose other than to cause visitors to wonder where they should sit.

"Just move those over to the side," she said, apparently anticipating my confusion.

Before we could sit down, the man stormed into the living room. He looked like someone used to getting his own way. He was bald except for a tuft of hair on the back of his head. "You let 'em in? Are you out of your mind?"

She was still staring at me. "This is Adam."

He looked confused. "Like from the Bible?"

"No, our grandson, Adam."

After a second or two it sank in. "This is Adam? After all these years? I can't believe it." He leaned against the nearest chair. "Why didn't you tell me it was Adam?"

"I just did."

"I mean earlier."

"I didn't know earlier."

"No matter," he said, turning his attention to me. "What are you doing here? How did you find us?"

"I'm on a mission for my church. The Mormons."

He nodded his head. "We used to live in Utah, for a short time. We moved back East about a year after . . . after . . ."

" . . . your mother died," she said, finishing his sentence.

"Do you remember her at all?" he asked.

"No, I'm sorry, I don't."

"No reason why you should. She died when you were about a year old."

"I know."

"We're Eddie and Claire," he said.

"He found us, Eddie, so I'm pretty sure he knows our names."

"We're your grandparents," he said.

"I also think he knows that."

Eddie was tired of her kibitzing. "Don't you have something in the kitchen you need to fetch?"

She turned to go. "All right, I'll get something, but don't make a fool of yourself. I mean it, Eddie. Don't make me come back here and be embarrassed."

"You never give me credit for anything," he called out as she started for the kitchen.

"Just don't smother the boy, that's all I'm asking. He's not used to us."

"What's there to get used to?"

She practically ran into the kitchen.

Eddie came over and stood in front of me. "Adam . . . Adam . . ."

"I'm hurrying, Eddie, do you hear me?" my grandmother called out from the kitchen. "I'm not even putting ice in the water."

Eddie reached out and wrapped his arms around me. He drew me close. "My boy, my boy, is it really you? It's been so long." He held me tight against him. I could feel his bristly beard against my cheek, and his clothes smelled like old people.

Just then Claire rushed back into the living room, carrying a plate of cookies and four glasses of water on a tray. "What are you doing? I go away for one minute, and when I come back you're hugging the poor boy?"

He let go of me. "Why shouldn't I hug him? He's my only grandson."

"He doesn't even remember us."

"And that's my fault?"

"This is not the time for that, Eddie. Just sit down."

He kissed me on the cheek. "Welcome home, son."

"Would you leave the poor boy alone!"

He grumbled under his breath and sat down. We all sat down.

We were back to gracious living again. "So, how are your folks?" she asked politely, as if she had no memory of just having yelled at her husband.

"They're doing good." It was then I realized I hadn't introduced Norton. "Oh, this is Elder Norton. He's from Idaho. His dad grows potatoes."

Norton turned to me and asked quietly, "These are your grandparents?"

"Yes."

"How come they don't know you very well?"

"My real mom died when I was very young. My dad remarried. And then—"

"We moved back East," Claire said. "That's where we were from originally. This is the same house we were living in when Charly was born. We rented it out while we lived in Utah." To Norton, she added, "Oh, Charly is Adam's mother."

"We tried to stay in contact with you after we moved out here," Eddie said.

"But that didn't always work," Claire said. "I guess Lara didn't want to confuse you. I mean, you already had two sets of grandparents."

"Who's Lara?" Norton asked.

"She's my stepmom. Actually, she's the only mom I can remember."

"At first Lara was very good at including us in family occasions," Claire said. "But then . . ." Her voice trailed off.

Eddie reached over and took two cookies then passed the plate to me. "Eat all you want." He looked trim and fit for his age, except for a slightly protruding stomach.

I took a cookie.

"Take more," Eddie said, gesturing with his hand. "Claire's got boxes and boxes stashed in the house somewhere. Of course, only she knows where they are. She can't eat 'em because she might put on an ounce. So if she's not going to eat any of 'em, she thinks I shouldn't either."

"Oh, hush. We've got our grandson here, and all you can talk about is cookies?" Claire said.

"I'm just trying to put him at ease."

"That's what you call it?"

"This is such a good cookie!" I said, desperately trying to change the subject.

"And then there was the Mormon thing," Eddie said. "We aren't Mormons, but, of course, Lara and Sam were, and the other grandparents."

"Your real mother converted not long after she met your dad."

"I know," I said. "My dad told me all about it. When I was about ten years old, he started taking me fishing to the same

7

lake he took my mom before they were married. He talked to me about her while we fished . . . but then . . ."

"What?" Eddie and Claire asked together.

"My mom found out about him talking about Charly, I guess, because after that my dad didn't talk to me very much about my real mom."

"You have a brother, don't you? Clinton, is it? How's he doing?" Claire asked.

"It's Quentin. He's doing really well. He just left on a mission to Finland. I won't get a chance to see him until he gets back, so that's not so good."

"How long is this mission of yours? Is it like forever?"

That made me laugh. "No, it's just for two years. I'll be finished the last week in April."

"And then what?"

"I'll work for my dad this summer and I'll be starting at BYU in the fall. My mom filled out all the paperwork and sent it in and even made a few phone calls to get me accepted."

"What are you going to study?" Eddie asked.

"Information systems."

"What's that?"

"It has to do with computers. You know, programming, Web site design, things like that."

"Too complicated for me," Eddie said, shaking his head, "although we do have the Internet and I have finally learned how to send an e-mail letter."

"My dad sets up Web sites for small businesses. I started working for him in ninth grade."

Seeing me glance at the plate of cookies, Eddie handed me the plate. "Take all you want! I'll go fill the plate in a minute."

"We still have some of your mom's things from when she was growing up," Claire said. "Photos and such . . . if you're interested."

"I'd like to see them. The thing is, I don't know much

about her, just what my dad told me, but that was a long time ago. I'd like to see whatever you have."

"I'll go haul some photo albums down," Eddie said, standing up. "We keep them in Charly's room. Oh, I know what you're thinking. After all these years to still call it her room and have her things in it. But, really, it's not that much trouble. It's a big house, and we've never really needed that room. I don't know about Claire, but I go in there once in a while and, you know, think about her. She was our only child." He cleared his throat. "We never expected we'd outlive her." He moved toward the stairs. "I'll go get the albums."

Norton touched my arm. "We'll need to go soon if we're going to make it to our appointment tonight."

I nodded. "I'm afraid we won't be able to stay much longer today," I told Eddie when he returned.

"When can you come see us again?" Eddie asked.

"Well, let me look at our schedule," I said, reaching for my planner.

"Can I talk with you for a minute privately?" Norton asked me.

We went outside on the porch. "What's up?" I asked.

"How can you justify coming here again when it's out of our area?" he asked.

"These are my grandparents."

"I didn't come out here to attend your family reunions. You're a good missionary. You keep the mission rules. If you start breaking this mission rule, where's it going to stop? They'll still be your grandparents after you're released. You can come back here then and spend as much time as you want with them."

I thought about what he'd said, then sighed. "You're right. We can't come back. Let's go tell them."

By the time we returned, Claire had filled the plate of cookies and replaced our water with lemonade.

9

"You're in luck! Claire went into the vault and brought out the mother lode of cookies just for you two."

I cleared my throat. "We have to go now. I'm really sorry about this, but we won't be able to come back."

They were stunned. "Why not?" Claire asked.

"Each pair of missionaries is assigned a particular area where they're supposed to work. We're not supposed to leave our area."

"Adam, where is your area?" Claire asked.

"It's Morristown."

"But that's not very far away. Won't they let you come here once in a while?"

"I'm afraid not."

Claire thoughtfully picked up a cookie, but she didn't take a bite. "What if we came and visited you?"

"Well, that would be better, except they'd like us to be teaching about our beliefs instead of just visiting."

"Is there any rule against us going to Morristown and having you teach us about your beliefs there?" Claire asked.

I looked at Norton who thought about it and then shrugged his shoulders.

"I guess we could do that," I said.

"Let's do it then!" Eddie called out. "We'll just talk first and enjoy each others' company, and then you can teach us, and then we'll all go out to eat. How does that sound?"

"Where are we going to do this?" Norton asked.

"The church?" I suggested.

"No, let's not do that," Eddie said. "How about this? We'll get ourselves a motel room, and then it'll be more like you're coming to our home, except we'll have cable and a swimming pool. And Claire will bring cookies for you both."

The details were worked out as Eddie and Claire drove us back to our apartment in Morristown.

♦ ♦ ♦

Our first meeting took place a week later at an upscale motel in Morristown. When we arrived, Eddie was waiting for us in the lobby.

He couldn't stop talking as he led us to the room. "Such a nice place. They have a pool, so you can go swimming if you want. And there's a sauna too. Also, did you know we're not far from where General George Washington camped during the Revolutionary War? So, it's really quite historic here. We can go there if you want. Of course we don't have to. Whatever you want."

Eddie put his hand on my shoulder as we continued down the hall to the room. "We got here an hour ago. Claire wanted to make it more like a home. Oh, and she brought some scrapbooks about your mother. And some of her paintings. Charly was an artist, you know. Also, we thought we'd have dinner delivered here. I hope you both like Chinese. Anyway, if we eat here, then it'll be more like home, you know what I'm saying?"

Eddie stopped at a door and knocked. "Claire, the boys are here."

When she opened the door, she saw his hand on my shoulder. "You've been smothering the boy again, haven't you?"

Eddie took his hand off my shoulder. "I most certainly have not been smothering the boy."

"Please come in," Claire said. "I'm sorry about my husband. We talked about this all the way over here, and I thought we had an agreement, but—"

"Who could blame me?" Eddie said. "I'm with my only grandson . . . after all these years."

Norton and I stepped inside. It was an expensive suite with a small living room and a hallway leading to the bedroom and a bathroom. On a coffee table were two scrapbooks

11

and a plate of cookies. And next to the table, propped against the wall, were some framed paintings.

"Sit down, relax, make yourself at home," Eddie said. "Have a cookie. In fact, I think we all should have a cookie."

I sat down on the couch between Claire and Eddie, and Norton took one of the big easy chairs.

"Would you like to look through the scrapbooks?" Claire asked.

I picked up the first scrapbook and opened it. On the first page was a photo of a newborn baby.

"That's your mom just after she was born," Claire said.

"I took the picture," Eddie said.

"She doesn't have any hair," I said. "I didn't either."

"We know. We were there," Claire said.

"Oh, right. I keep forgetting."

"I can see her in you," Claire said. "Same color eyes and hair."

"You've got her smile too," Eddie said.

Over the next hour I went through the two scrapbooks, watching my mother grow from a baby to where she was in high school. Norton grew restless and bored. Without the cookies, he'd have never made it.

They showed me the paintings Charly had done. They were modernistic, filled with bold strokes and lots of bright colors.

"Do you have more things of hers?" I asked, while I held up one of the paintings, which Claire explained Charly had done when she was not much older than me.

"We do," Claire said. "We'll bring them the next time we visit."

"What was she like growing up?"

"Oh, she was a handful," Eddie laughed. "Like with the harp lessons. In junior high, she insisted on taking harp lessons. So we bought her a harp. She took a few lessons and then gave it up. Do you have any idea what kind of a loss you

12

can take trying to sell a used harp? I couldn't bear to let it go for what people were willing to pay for it, so we still have it."

"When she was your age, she loved life, and she loved people," Claire said. "And, she was . . . well . . . exuberant . . . and unpredictable."

"When your dad first met her, that was the one thing about her he couldn't stand," Eddie added.

"But it was exactly what your dad needed," Claire said. "Before Charly came along, he was more driven by duty. Oh, he was polite, of course, but some people love people, and some just put up with 'em. Your dad spent more time thinking about what was the right thing to do, but very little time enjoying life."

"That's the way he is now," I said.

"He was a different person when he was around your mother," Claire said.

"Like when he got arrested in New York City," Eddie said.

"My dad got arrested in New York City?"

"Didn't he ever tell you about that?" Eddie asked with a big grin.

"No, but I'd love to hear the story."

Eddie leaned closer and spoke confidentially. "Well, after your mom converted to a Mormon, she and your dad were dating quite seriously. But then your dad found out a few things about your mom that had happened before he met her and, well, the truth is, he said something to her that was very cruel."

"It was more insensitive than cruel," Claire corrected.

"What did my dad say?"

Eddie and Claire looked at each other, then Claire shook her head.

"It's not important," Eddie said. "Anyway, your mom flew back East to continue her studies. Eventually your dad realized what a jerk he'd been and how much he cared about your mom, so he flew back to talk to her. He tried to patch things

13

up, but she would have none of it. So your dad barged into a place he had no business being and got himself arrested by New York's finest. As far as I can tell, that was the only spontaneous thing that poor boy had ever done his entire life. But, what can I say? He was in love. It made no sense, it wasn't part of his plans, it wasn't like him to act so impulsively, but, that's okay. What she'd done before she met your dad didn't matter."

"That's a great story!" I said.

"We've got a lot more of 'em," Eddie said, grinning.

Norton cleared his throat and glanced at his watch.

I nodded. "This has really been great to look at these pictures, but, right now, could we teach you about our beliefs?"

"Yes, of course. Let me get these things out of your way," Claire said, picking up the scrapbooks and setting them on the floor next to the door.

Our first discussion went amazingly well. So well, in fact, that it seemed like they already knew the material. "Have you been taught before by the missionaries?" I asked.

"No, but, if you can believe it, Mister Information Systems, I did go to your church's Web site and print out some information about your beliefs," Eddie said proudly.

"It took him half the day to do it," Claire said good-naturedly, "but to his credit, he didn't give up. And, finally, he learned how to do it."

"We studied all week," Eddie said.

"Why?"

"We didn't want you to have any reason not to keep teaching us. Did we do okay? Will you teach us again?" Claire asked.

Norton and I were in shock. "Yes, for sure, let's do this again in a few days," I said.

Just then there was a knock on the door. It was a delivery guy with two big plastic bags containing several cartons of Chinese food. Norton had forgotten we were going to have

14

dinner and just about had a fit that we had been there so long. That didn't keep him from wolfing down his share, though. But as soon as he was finished he reminded me we needed to be on our way.

As we said our thanks and were preparing to leave, I asked Claire if she would say the closing prayer.

"If you want me to do it, I will," Claire said.

Norton taught some basics about how to pray and then we all knelt down.

"Father in Heaven?" Claire said tentatively.

"We thank thee," Norton said softly.

"We thank thee . . . that we can spend time . . . with our grandson. He is such a fine boy. His mother would be so proud of him . . ." She stopped.

"Claire, you okay?" Eddie asked.

"I just had a feeling, that's all," she said. She stood up. "Excuse me, I need to get some tissues."

A minute later she returned with some tissues. She knelt back down. "Where were we?" she asked Norton.

"We ask thee . . ." Norton prompted.

"We ask thee to help Eddie and me understand these things . . ." She paused.

"I'm done. How do I stop my prayer?"

◆　　◆　　◆

For the next few weeks we met every Wednesday at the same time in the same suite. They couldn't seem to get enough of what they were learning. Norton and I were amazed at the progress they were making.

In fact, we were so excited that, at the next zone conference, the second Wednesday in February, during sharing time, Norton said, "There's this older couple we're teaching who actually download our beliefs from the Church's Web

15

site and study it so they'll be prepared for us when we come to teach them."

"That's incredible!" President McNamara said. He leaned forward. "I would love to meet these people. Where do they live?"

"They live in Madison," Norton said.

I cringed, hoping President McNamara wouldn't connect that Madison wasn't in our area. I also hoped that the elders who were working in Madison would just let it go and talk to me after the meeting. I was sure we could work something out. No use involving the mission president in this tiny little detail.

Sister Doneau raised her hand. "Elder Norton, how is it that you're teaching investigators who live in our area, and yet Sister Bagley and I don't know anything about it?"

"We don't teach them in your area," Norton said. "They come to Morristown once a week."

"I see. I'm curious why you would encourage people to leave our area so they can be taught by you and your companion."

Elder Norton looked flustered. "You'll have to talk to Elder Roberts about that."

"Elder Roberts?" President McNamara asked.

I turned and faced Sister Doneau's humorless gaze. She was a legend in the mission. Everyone knew she was only twenty-three but had already completed a law degree from Columbia Law School before coming on her mission. I had once seen her demolish a zone leader when he tried to over-play his authority and impose an unfair restriction on the sisters.

"Elder Roberts," she said, "I would be very interested in knowing how you justify teaching our people in your area."

"I'd be happy to explain that to you, Sister, but I'm not sure this is the right time for that. We have so few opportunities to hear from President and Sister McNamara. I'm sure

16

we don't want to take away from their time to give us counsel and direction. Unless you don't care about hearing from our leaders—"

"President McNamara, would it be possible for the four of us to meet with you to discuss this matter?" Doneau interrupted.

The president nodded. "Yes, of course, let's get together after this meeting."

"We have a teaching appointment at six-thirty," Norton said.

"Someone from *our* area, Elder?" Doneau asked with a pleasant smile that wasn't fooling me one bit.

"No."

As the meeting continued, Norton and I watched as Sister Doneau bent over a notebook, furiously writing out her thoughts.

"She's going to demolish us," Norton quietly moaned.

"I'm not afraid of her."

"You should be. Everyone else is."

"We haven't done anything wrong," I said. "We're teaching them in our area."

"The first time we visited them we were out of our area."

"Well, that's true, but that was only the one time."

"Right, only one time."

Norton glanced over at Sister Doneau. "Look at her," he whispered, "preparing to argue her case before the Supreme Court, and here we are, cowering in our seats."

"We're not cowering in our seats."

I couldn't take my eyes off her for the rest of the meeting. To me Sister Doneau looked like someone you'd get to play the lead in an action-adventure movie. She might have been pretty, if she had taken any interest in her appearance. But she wore no makeup, and her shoulder-length brown hair hung straight down without so much as a hint of curl to it. With her high cheekbones, at a glance you might imagine she was part

Indian. She didn't smile a lot, and as one of the elders said of her, "She takes no prisoners."

The small, wire-rim glasses she wore made her look much more intelligent than she could possibly be. Also, her eyebrows. My gosh, it was like a forest in there.

Instead of military fatigues, which is what the rest of her appearance cried out for, she wore a plain white blouse, buttoned high on her neck, and a long, straight gray skirt.

She must have been aware of my gaze, because near the end of the meeting, she gave me a condescending smile and held up her notebook for me to see. Then she slowly tapped it on her hand like it was a loaded weapon.

"You're right," I whispered to Norton. "We're in big trouble."

2

After zone conference ended, President McNamara told us he had a few more interviews before he could meet with us. Within minutes, the meetinghouse halls were deserted except for Doneau and her companion, Sister Bagley, a dewy-eyed, soft-spoken new missionary who was both shy and yet strangely intense in her religious fervor, and Norton and me, cocky on the outside but very much worried about tangling with Brianna Doneau.

Ordinarily I wouldn't have known a sister missionary's first name, but throughout the mission she was called "Brianna, Be Brief!" by the elders unfortunate enough to have ever served in the same district with her. She had the nickname because once she had her mind set on something, she'd press her arguments until she wore everybody down.

While Doneau sat and studied the notes she'd prepared for our meeting with the president, I paced the floor. "This is taking too long. Norton and I have work to do."

Doneau looked up. "Let me see if I understand—what you and Elder Norton have to do is very important, but what

19

Sister Bagley and I have planned for tonight is of no value. Is that how you see it, Elder?"

Our companions were staring at us. I so much wanted to say something mean, but for Sister Bagley's sake, I held back. "Not at all, Sister. We're all in this work together."

She smiled politely. I suspected she might have wanted to unleash some law school rhetoric on me, but to her credit, she didn't do it, maybe for the same reason I hadn't said anything. "I appreciate that, Elder."

I sat down next to her. "I'm curious about something. Since you already have a law degree, why did you even come on a mission? You could be making a pile of money right now."

"I wanted my life to count for something."

"Oh, sure, and also because you weren't married, right?"

I meant it as a harmless joke, so I wasn't prepared for how she took it. For some reason I'd hit a nerve.

"Sorry. I was just joking around," I said.

She recovered quickly enough to come back at me. "Is that your opinion of all sister missionaries, Elder Roberts?"

"Well, no, not really. I was just—"

"Just me then, right? Look, I don't need to justify to you, or to anyone else, why I came on a mission. And another thing—I don't see that my personal life is any of your concern."

"Sorry. I was just trying to start a conversation, but I can see you'd rather be left alone." I stood up and walked away.

For the next few minutes, I pretended to ignore her, but I kept stealing glances at her. I felt sorry for her. Nobody in the mission liked her. At least none of the elders in any area she'd ever been in.

She's so in-your-face about everything, I thought. *Everyone just puts up with her. I bet that's the way it's always been.*

Although she irked me, I felt guilty for what I'd said. *She*

20

probably came on a mission for the same reason most people come, the same reason I came.

I'd grown up with my mom encouraging me to be nice. I knew she would not approve of the way I'd treated Sister Doneau, so, after a few minutes, I walked over to her again. "You know what? I need to apologize for what I said."

At first she gave me an icy stare, but then, as she decided my apology was sincere, her expression softened. "Thank you for saying that."

We made eye contact. She had an ivory complexion and an interesting combination of dark brown hair and blue eyes. In high school I'd once told a friend I wanted to find a girl with brown hair and blue eyes. He'd told me nobody had brown hair and blue eyes. And now, standing in front of her, I was surprised there was anything to like about her. I kept staring at her. And then, after a few seconds, we both panicked. I turned away, and she escaped down the hall.

I felt like an idiot. I worried she'd think I liked her. I thought of going after her and telling her I didn't, but somehow that didn't seem like the polite thing to do. So I let it go.

A few minutes later President McNamara opened the door and two elders left. He called out to me. "Elder Roberts, what time did you say your appointment is?" He motioned the four of us to come into the stake president's office he was using for interviews.

"Six-thirty," I said as we sat down and he closed the door.

He looked at his watch. "Maybe we should reschedule then."

"This shouldn't take long, President McNamara," Doneau said brusquely. "If it meets with your approval, I would like to read a prepared statement, and then we can proceed."

"Yes, by all means, Sister Doneau," I said. "I'm sure we're all waiting for your prepared statement, which you so carefully crafted during President McNamara's inspiring closing message to us."

Doneau continued to glance over her notes, but then, realizing that everyone was waiting for her to respond, she looked over at me and asked, "I'm sorry, Elder, did you say something?"

I gave her a fake smile. "Nothing important, Sister Doneau."

President McNamara, who had already put in a long day, sighed at having yet one more mountain to climb. "We'd better pray before we start. Elder Roberts, will you offer the prayer?"

In my prayer, I said, "Please help us resolve this so my grandparents can continue to be taught the missionary lessons."

After the prayer, President McNamara said, "Elder Roberts, did I hear you correctly? It's your grandparents you're teaching?"

I told him the whole story, then added, "I'm pretty sure the reason they agreed to have us teach them is so they can spend some time with me."

"That may be true," Doneau said, "but as I see it, the main issue here is the sovereignty of missionary areas. In fact, if I may read my prepared statement—"

The president cut her off. "Sister Doneau, I don't believe it's necessary for you to continue. It's abundantly clear to me that these good people should not have to leave their home and rent a motel room in order to be taught the gospel. Of course they should be taught in their own home."

Doneau glanced at me and smirked. "I totally agree, President. I assume you'll want us to teach them, since they do live in our area."

"President, I'm not sure they'll continue without me," I countered. "I would very much like to be there for the discussions."

"Even if Sister Doneau and Sister Bagley are doing the teaching?" President McNamara asked.

I wanted to say, "*Especially* if they're doing the teaching," but I didn't because it would have only made things worse. Even so, the long pause probably gave me away.

"Elder?" President McNamara asked.

"I'm sure Sister Doneau and Sister Bagley do an excellent job teaching, President, but . . . well, these are my grandparents, so, naturally I want everything to go well. I'm sure you understand."

President McNamara leaned back in his seat, clasped his fingers together, placed them behind his head, and looked up at the ceiling as he tried to come up with his decision.

A minute later, he put his hands on the desk and turned in my direction. "Elder Roberts," President McNamara said, "I can see why you'd want to be with your grandparents for the discussions, and so I will give you and Elder Norton permission to travel to your grandparents' home in Madison once a week for a missionary discussion. I want the lesson to be taught jointly by both sets of missionaries. You may stay half an hour after the discussion, Elders, and then you are to return to your own area."

"But, President," Doneau complained, "I haven't read my prepared statement yet."

He stood up. "We're done here, Sister Doneau."

We all had the same train to catch. Doneau was so mad at me she wouldn't even walk with us. She and Sister Bagley stayed half a block ahead of us. I didn't care. The fact is, I preferred it.

I'm sure that Doneau wanted to beat us to the station, grab the next train, and leave us behind. But we all ended up getting to the station just after the train pulled out, so we had half an hour to kill.

Doneau tried to stay away from us but, for some reason, I couldn't let it go.

I approached her and her companion.

"On Friday we're meeting again with my grandparents. I'd

like to teach them about the importance of baptism. If it's okay with you guys, I'll get us started. When we come to a scripture, I'll ask one of you to read it, and bear your testimony."

"I was under the impression we'd all have a chance to teach," Doneau said icily.

"We will."

"What would you like Sister Bagley to teach?"

"Sister Bagley, how about if you give the opening prayer?"

"All right," Sister Bagley said.

"How is she going to get better unless she has a chance to teach?" Doneau asked.

"How about if she practices on your investigators and not on my grandparents?"

"So, basically, you're going to do most of the teaching while the rest of us sit around admiring you. Is that the way you see this? Well, in my opinion, that's not fair. I'm certain President McNamara intended that Sister Bagley and I do the teaching, with you and your companion responding when asked. After all, they do live in our area."

"We've been teaching them, so they're used to us."

"I don't see how anyone could ever get used to you, Elder. And another thing, quit staring at me all the time."

"What are you talking about?"

"You *know* what I'm talking about."

I turned to Sister Bagley. "Your companion is delusional."

Sister Bagley looked like she was going to cry. "Would Heavenly Father want us to be so mean to each other?"

Doneau and I each waited for the other to apologize. So neither one of us said anything. Finally, I walked off.

After a few minutes, Sister Bagley came to me privately. "We'll need the Spirit when we teach your grandparents."

"You know how unreasonable she is sometimes," I complained.

"Maybe if we have a prayer, it'll help," Bagley said.

24

"We are not going to have a prayer here with people all around us," I said. "That would be way too weird."

"Then I think you need to apologize," Bagley said.

I actually considered apologizing. It was something my mom would have encouraged me to do.

But I waited too long. The train was coming.

Bagley had made a good point. We'd never get anywhere trying to teach if there was contention between us.

"I'll call you tonight so we can get this straightened out," I said to Doneau. "I'll call about nine."

"We'll still be out teaching," Doneau said. "We're so busy these days."

"Yeah, right," I scoffed.

"Don't call me tonight," she said. "I don't want to talk to you."

The train stopped. We watched Doneau and Bagley climb aboard one car. We boarded the next car.

That night I phoned the sisters. Bagley told me Doneau wouldn't talk to me.

"Then tell her something for me. Tell her I'm sorry if I hurt her feelings."

There was a long pause while the message was relayed.

"She says that isn't enough."

"Why isn't it enough?"

Another long pause.

"Because you're only apologizing because you think that . . ." Bagley had to stop to get prompted. " . . . you have to do it rather than . . . admitting how bullheaded . . . unreasonable . . . and totally impossible to get along with you are."

"Do you find me unreasonable, Sister Bagley?"

Long pause. "Not really."

"Tell her that," I said.

Another long pause. "I don't think so."

"I understand. You have to live with her."

"It's not that bad most of the time."

Doneau must have figured out what we were talking about. She came on the line. "I will not have you bad-mouthing me to my companion," she said, her voice low and threatening.

"Why not? Everyone else in the mission does."

She hung up.

Once again, after a short time, I regretted what I'd said. I tried to call several times that night, but apparently they'd taken their phone off the hook.

On Friday morning, the day we were going to give another discussion, I asked Norton what he thought I should do.

Norton shrugged. "Give Doneau whatever she wants."

"Just cave in to her demands? Why would I do that?"

"Because if you don't, our time with your grandparents is going to be a total disaster."

"I'm not going to let her walk all over me."

"Then we might as well not show up tonight," he said.

I paced the floor, shaking my head. "It isn't fair."

"What other choice have you got? You can't change her. So, between you two, who's left?"

I raged against the injustice of having to let her have her way, but by the time we met Doneau and Bagley at the train station in Madison that night, I'd resigned myself to do what Norton had suggested.

"Sister Doneau, I'm sorry for what I said on the phone. Also, I want you to know that I've changed my mind. You tell us what you want to happen tonight, and we'll go along with that."

"Sister Bagley and I will do whatever you say, Elder Roberts," she said sweetly, with none of the animosity that had been there before between us.

"What's going on here?"

"I decided this was a time where I should honor the priesthood."

26

Very clever ploy, I thought. *Brilliant strategy. She has me where she wants me. Now I'll have to act reasonably . . . and be fair.*

"How about if I summarize what Elder Norton and I covered last time, and then you start the discussion. Whenever you want, just nod to Norton and he'll carry on, and then Sister Bagley, and then you again. I'll summarize, then ask one of them to offer a prayer."

She nodded. "That sounds like a very good plan."

"Thank you."

We were staring into each other's eyes again, this time trying to figure out what had caused the change in the other.

"Why did you give up?" I asked her privately.

"This is too important to mess up," she said.

"Thank you."

I had previously called my grandparents and told them two sister missionaries would be with us, so they were expecting them.

We met in their living room. We spent the first half hour giving the sisters a chance to get acquainted with Eddie and Claire and looking through scrapbooks. Doneau and Bagley learned all about my mom and dad.

"Charly had a way of helping Sam break out of his usual boring and predictable lifestyle," Claire said. "She was so spontaneous and freewheeling, and he was so reserved, that it was a wonder they got along at all." She laughed and shook her head, "At times she'd embarrass him horribly, and he'd get frustrated with her; but, on the other hand, she filled his life with fun."

"I'd like to be more like that someday," Doneau said. "I tend to be direct and goal-oriented."

"You're more like Sam, then. Adam, I mean Elder Roberts, what are you like?" Claire asked.

"I'm more like my dad. He's driven by goals. My mom is like that, too, come to think of it."

27

"Sister Bagley?"

"I'm not much fun either."

"Elder Norton?"

"I'm the same way."

"Well, let's stick together and see how we all change," Claire said cheerily.

Eddie reached down next to the sofa and retrieved a baseball mitt and held it out to me. "There you go . . . son."

"What's this?" I asked.

"Just a little something. I bought it for you the day you were born. At the time, Claire told me I'd better wait until you were a little older before I gave it to you." He cleared his throat. "I guess I waited too long. Before we even knew it, your mom got sick, and then . . . well . . ."

He stopped talking and stared at the floor. I thought Claire would step in and get us through this, but she didn't. She was getting teary-eyed too.

"The thing is, everybody lost out in this deal," Eddie continued. "You lost your mom, your dad lost the love of his life, but . . ." he cleared his throat. " . . . Claire and I lost too. We lost the chance to be your granddaddy and your grandmomma, and to spoil you rotten like we wanted to . . . and to always be on your side, no matter what curves life threw you. That's what we lost."

He handed me the baseball glove. "I suppose you're a little too old to play Little League ball now, aren't you? Well, save it for when you have a boy, then at least he'll get some use out of it."

"Thank you," I stammered. I held the mitt in one hand and grabbed his hand with my other and held it tightly for a moment.

"Oh, there's an electric train too, stored away in the basement," Eddie said.

By this time Doneau and Bagley had tears in their eyes also.

28

"Look at us, bawling our eyes out like this," Claire finally said. She got up and went into the bathroom then came back with a box of tissues. We each took one, except for Norton, who seemed to be lost in his own world.

From that point on, I never again thought of them as Eddie and Claire. They became, to me, my grandfather and my grandmother. The way they loved me after all the years, with little or no contact, made it easy to love them too.

"We'd probably better get started," Norton said.

Our presentation about the importance of baptism went better than I'd hoped for. I had to admit Doneau did a good job teaching.

Afterwards, my grandfather, with some help from Sister Doneau, said the prayer. As we were about to leave, my grandmother said, "Don't go yet. We have dessert."

"Claire made her famous Italian dessert," my grandfather said. "Just sit and relax. It'll only take a minute."

Claire started toward the kitchen. Eddie looked like he wanted to stay, but Claire, probably worried he'd give me a hug, called for him to help her.

As he stood up to leave, Doneau asked what dessert she'd fixed.

"I'm pretty sure it's tiramisu," he said. "That's what she usually fixes for company." With that, he left.

"Tiramisu is made with coffee and wine," Doneau whispered frantically, panic written on her face.

"Are you serious?" I asked.

"What are we going to do?" Bagley asked.

My grandfather came back with a tray of glasses of water. "Claire got up real early this morning to make this, so I sure hope you enjoy it." He set out our drinks and then returned to the kitchen.

"How can we eat this if it's got coffee and wine in it?" Doneau whispered to me.

"It probably doesn't have much," I said quietly.

"So what are you saying? A little coffee and wine is okay? Is that it?" Doneau replied.

"What I'm saying is, this is my grandmother, and she went to a lot of work to make this for us, and I really don't see how we can offend her by not having any."

"So what if she offers us a beer next time?" Doneau hissed. "Are we going to chugalug that down too?"

"Could you possibly be reasonable for once in your life? We're talking about a tiny piece of dessert."

"This isn't about being reasonable," she said.

"What is it about then?"

"Why are you so willing to throw away everything you've been taught your entire life? Do you have any actual guiding principles in your life or not?"

Just then, my grandparents came in with Claire carrying a tray of dessert on small plates.

"Here it is!" my grandfather announced. "You're going to love this!"

Eddie took the tray, and my grandmother handed each of us a plate. Doneau and I traded desperate glances.

I was not going to offend my grandmother and so I took a small bite. It was the best dessert I had ever had in my life. "This is so good! It doesn't taste at all like . . . what I thought it would taste like."

Doneau sighed and took a tiny bite, then broke into a big smile. "Oh, my gosh, that is *amazing!*" she said.

Norton was the next to go. "Wow," he said.

Finally Bagley took a taste. "This tastes real good!" she said in her little girl voice.

"Eat it up, children. There's plenty more in the kitchen," my grandmother said.

"I'm afraid if I eat too much, I won't be able to sleep tonight," Doneau said.

Total silence.

"Why's that?" my grandmother asked.

30

"Well," Doneau said, "isn't there coffee in tiramisu?"

"Tiramisu? This isn't tiramisu. It's cannoli. Who told you it was tiramisu?"

Eddie nervously smiled. "You always make tiramisu for company."

"Not for the missionaries. What is wrong with you? Missionaries don't use coffee or wine. This just has ricotta and chocolate in it."

"I'll have some more then!" Norton said.

We each had seconds.

"This is so good!" Doneau said. "Is there any chance I could get the recipe?"

"Oh, yes, of course," my grandmother said.

The sisters went into the kitchen with my grandmother. I went through yet another scrapbook with my grandfather, and Norton had some more dessert.

It was amazing to see my mother when she was about the same age as me. I could see why my dad had fallen in love with her.

We could hear the sisters and my grandmother laughing a few times during the time they were gone. I was glad they were getting along so well.

My grandmother insisted we take some dessert with us and gave each of us a piece in a plastic container. We were all very grateful.

"This has been so nice to be with you both today," Doneau said.

"Can all four of you come back for our next lesson?" my grandfather asked. "Tell us what it's going to be about and we'll prepare for it."

"Yes, we can do that."

"Would it be all right if Sister Bagley and I drop by once in a while when we're in the area?" Doneau asked.

"By all means. Come by anytime," Claire said.

"Next time come a little earlier, and I'll cook up some

31

steaks," my grandfather said. "We've got an outdoor grill now, and I've become quite the master chef."

"In his mind at least," my grandmother teased.

"Do we have to call you *sister* all the time?" my grandfather asked.

"I'm afraid you do."

"Well, tell me this and I promise not to tell a soul. What's your first name?"

"I really can't tell you," Doneau said.

"It's Brianna," I said without thinking.

Doneau glared at me, then turned to my grandparents. "Please don't call me that though."

"We won't," my grandmother said, turning to my grandfather so he'd know he'd been warned. "We want you to feel comfortable while you're in our home."

Once again, as the four of us headed back to the train station, Doneau, with Bagley trying to keep up with her, forged on ahead of us.

We had a ten-minute wait for the train. At first Doneau ignored us, but then she marched over to me and said, "We need to talk."

We walked a few feet away from our companions. "How do you know my first name?" she asked.

"One of the elders in your last area told me."

"How did he know?"

"I'd rather not say."

"You'd better tell me," she demanded.

"Well . . . some of the elders in the mission call you 'Brianna, Be Brief.'"

She gasped. "Why would they call me that?"

I tried to put a positive spin to it. "Because you stand up for yourself, but that's good, you know, that you don't let people walk all over you. I should be more like that."

"What else do they say about me?" she demanded.

32

"That you have a law degree and . . . that sometimes you're just . . . a tiny bit difficult to work with."

"They say I'm hard to work with? Well, I think you can see that simply isn't true."

As a joke I faked the look of a browbeaten husband. "Yes, dear, whatever you say."

"Don't call me dear."

"Relax, okay? Can't you tell when someone is being sarcastic?"

"You *are* interested in me, aren't you?"

"No, not a bit," I said. "For your information, I have someone waiting for me. She's very good-looking and always treats me with a great deal of respect."

Actually, that was a lie. There was nobody waiting for me, at least not by that point in my mission. The girls I'd been friends with in high school were now all getting married. I said it just to keep Doneau from thinking I cared about her, which I truly did not.

"I have someone waiting for me too," she said.

"Well, I hope he waits."

"Oh, he'll wait, don't you worry about that," she shot back. "He's totally committed to our relationship."

"I'm very happy for your relationship," I said pleasantly.

"We will not talk about this again, will we," she said. It was not a question.

"I certainly hope not."

We returned to our companions.

◆　　◆　　◆

When we arrived for our next visit, my grandfather had the electric train he had bought for me when I was a baby, set up in the living room. We watched it make its way around the circular track and then he handed me the controls. "Go ahead, give it a try."

It was embarrassing to be doing this in front of Norton, Bagley, and Doneau, but for my grandfather's sake, I did my best to be enthusiastic about the train.

"This is really great!"

"It's all yours," my grandfather said proudly. "This is the first time it's ever been used."

"I would've gotten a big kick out of this when I was a kid," I said.

"That's for sure," my grandfather said. And then he got misty-eyed again, and in a lower voice, added, "There's a lot of things we could've done together, just you and me. And of course other things with Claire and me and you." He shook his head. "But that's all water under the bridge now, right? We've got to move on."

He looked so sad, I didn't care if the others were watching. I reached over and rested my hand on his arm. "I wish we could've done those things . . . Grandfather."

He swallowed hard. "That's something I've always wanted to hear," he said.

"I can call you that now . . . if you want."

He looked at my hand on his arm and nodded. "I would appreciate that."

I turned to my grandmother. "What would you like me to call you, Claire?"

She smiled. "I would like it if you called me Grand-mother."

"I'll do that."

"Group hug?" my grandfather suggested.

"That sounds like a great idea," I said.

The three of us stood up and put our arms around each other like a small football team in a huddle.

I was very happy at that moment.

Maybe too happy. I looked at Doneau and said, "Care to join us?"

34

She laughed. "Well, I'm not going to hug you, that's for sure, but I can hug your grandmother. How would that be?"

My grandmother and Doneau hugged each other, and then they invited Sister Bagley to join them.

Norton glanced at Eddie then looked over at me and just held up his hands in a defensive gesture.

Doneau taught most of the lesson and did a good job. My grandparents even agreed to go to church on Sunday.

A week later, one day before we were scheduled to teach my grandparents again, Doneau called. "Guess what? Today when we dropped by, your grandparents asked about tithing, so we taught them. It went really well."

I was stunned.

"Are you still there?" she asked.

"I thought we'd agreed that we were all going to teach together."

"Well, we dropped by to see them, and they started asking about it, and before we knew it, we'd taught them."

"I see," I said icily.

"If you want, we can go over the same material when you and your companion are with us," Doneau said.

"No, that won't be necessary."

"How about if you do most of the teaching next time?" she asked.

"I think that's a good idea."

The next day when we met with my grandparents, I started out doing the teaching, but my grandparents directed most of their questions to Doneau.

Afterwards we had cannoli again, but this time Doneau and Bagley had made it. They'd spent the afternoon in the kitchen with my grandmother.

I was depressed that it tasted so good.

"What do you think?" my grandmother asked.

"It's okay, I guess," I said with little enthusiasm.

"The best part was us being able to work with you in the kitchen," Doneau told my grandmother.

After we finished eating, my grandfather asked the four of us what I at first thought was a strange question. "How are things in your apartments? Does everything work where you live?"

"What do you mean?" I asked.

"Do the drains drain? Are the faucets leaking? Do the locks work? Anything needing fixing? Because if there is, I'd be happy to drop over sometime and fix whatever isn't working. It's what I do every day. Come on out to the garage and I'll show you around."

"Sisters, don't go out there. It's boring. Let's stay here and talk," my grandmother said.

Norton and I went to the garage with my grandfather. He showed us all the tools he had, and more nuts, bolts, and screws in neatly labeled bins than most hardware stores carried.

Norton wasn't much interested, so he went just outside the garage and looked at the garden.

"I've changed a lot since we lived in Utah," my grandfather said. "Back then I was a corporate star. In fact, your Grandfather Roberts was one of my coworkers. I'll tell you sometime how, in a way, I was responsible for your dad and your mom meeting, but not now." He sighed. "When your mom died, I felt like my whole world had been shot out from under me. I couldn't work with the same energy I used to have. Nothing seemed to matter anymore. So, after a while, I resigned, and we moved back here, where we had lived while Charly was growing up."

He opened up a metal drawer and pulled out some bolts and gently tossed them in his hand while he continued. "I didn't work for a year, and then I heard about an apartment building for sale. It needed a lot of work, and the owner had been trying to sell it for a while. It was in a good neighborhood, and I felt it could bring in some money if it were completely remodeled. So I took out a loan and started to fix up the place. Within a year we started to make money."

He returned the bolts to the drawer and led me to an area where he kept his plumbing supplies. "At first none of the people who lived there trusted me because the previous owner had let the place go downhill. But after a while, they learned that I'd be there if they had a problem. Now, even with three apartment buildings, I take great pride in taking care of my tenants, fixing their toilets, their drains, their faucets, painting, planting flowers in the spring, fertilizing the lawns, keeping up the grounds. They know they can count on me when there's a problem."

Norton peeked into the garage. "Elder, we need to be going now."

My grandfather offered to give us rides back to our apartments, but we told him it would be better for us if we took the train.

As the four of us walked back to the train station, I spoke to Doneau. "I want you to quit dropping by and seeing them all the time."

"I can't agree to that," Doneau said.

"I knew this was a big mistake to let you two into the teaching process."

"They live in our area. If we want to visit them every fifteen minutes, we'll do it," she retorted.

"I want to be there when they're taught."

"Why? Are you implying we don't do a good job? How can you say that after having seen me teach?"

"It's easy, actually." The minute I said it, I regretted it. But I wasn't going to back down.

"You don't care anything about my feelings, do you?" Doneau asked.

"You don't have feelings, Doneau. You're a lawyer, for crying out loud."

"I have feelings."

"Well what about my feelings?" I blurted out. "Are they of no importance to you?"

Now I can see that what I said could be misinterpreted. What I meant, of course, was that these were my grandparents and I wanted to be there whenever they were taught.

Unfortunately, Norton and Bagley heard my outburst. They both looked at me with suspicion.

"I can't talk to you anymore without my companion," Doneau said, returning to Bagley.

When the train came, we again boarded different cars.

Later that night, Norton asked, "So, what's going on between you and Doneau?"

"Nothing is going on. I'm just mad at her for taking over everything."

Two days later I got a phone call from President McNamara. "We're transferring you today, Elder." He gave me the details. I was being transferred to the farthest end of the mission and was to get on the earliest bus available.

"Why am I being transferred?"

"I think you probably know the answer to that."

"I haven't done anything wrong."

"We'll talk about it next zone conference. But, for now, you're being transferred to an area where there are no sisters."

I phoned the sisters. Sister Doneau answered.

"You got me transferred, didn't you?" I asked.

"What are you talking about?"

"I'm being transferred today. You wanted me out of the picture, didn't you, so you'd be the one to teach and baptize my grandparents? You called President McNamara, didn't you?"

There was a long pause. "I did call him, but I didn't ask him to transfer you."

"What did you tell him?"

"I'd rather not say. But let me say this, I do hope you'll be able to be there when your grandparents are baptized."

"Oh, I'll be there, Sister Doneau, don't you worry about that."

"Even if it means breaking mission rules? That's what got you into this problem, isn't it?"

I hung up on her.

I turned to Norton. "Let's go visit my grandparents."

"That's out of our area."

"So what are they going to do? Transfer me? Let's go."

I packed and then we left.

By the time we arrived at my grandparents' place, I'd cooled down enough to realize I should not let them know how furious I was with Doneau for getting me transferred. I didn't want to put any barriers in the way of their continuing with the discussions.

First I explained that missionaries generally serve a few months in one area and then they're transferred. "Well, that's what's happening to me. I'm being transferred. I leave today. So I won't be around for a while."

My grandmother looked as though she was going to cry. "You're leaving?"

"I'm afraid so. But the sisters will continue teaching you."

"Who do we call to complain about you leaving?" my grandfather demanded.

I talked to them about sustaining Church leaders.

"Maybe we could come to church where you are when we get baptized," my grandfather said.

"That would be wonderful. There's nothing I'd like better." Then I let out a big sigh. "But . . . you need to be around the people in your ward, so they can help you."

"You are so much like Lara," my grandmother said.

"How's that?"

"You're very strict with yourself."

"I'll only be in my new area for a couple of months and

39

then my mission will be over. Before I go back West, I'll come and visit you."

"It's not fair," my grandmother said. "Your family in Utah has had you for twenty years. I think we should have you for at least a little while."

Norton tapped me on the sleeve and pointed to his watch.

I nodded and stood up. "We really need to go," I said. "I'm sorry about this. It's not the way I pictured this turning out. I hope this won't discourage you from continuing to learn about the Church." I felt as though I should bear my testimony to them.

"I want you to know that I know the things we have been teaching you are true. Joseph Smith really is a true prophet, and the Church is the kingdom of God on earth. There is nothing more important than you being baptized. Please keep studying with the sisters."

My grandfather cleared his throat. "For the past twenty years we've gone over in our minds the changes we saw in your mother when she joined the Church. At first, we weren't in favor of what she was doing, but as time went on, she became such a powerful influence on us that we began to think that maybe there is something to this, after all. What we've learned from what you've taught us has strengthened that conviction." He paused. "So we're going to go ahead with this."

"That is great news," I said softly.

"We're glad you were the one to teach us," my grandfather said. "You're all we have left of our daughter now. Before you go, there's something I want to give you. I'll be right back."

In spite of bad knees, he hurried up the stairs.

"Can I make you a sack lunch to take?" my grandmother asked. "I could make you some sandwiches."

"No, that's okay, I'll be fine. It's not a very long bus ride."

My grandfather returned carrying a photograph of my

real mom and my dad on the day they were married. "I found this last night. I thought you might like to have it."

I felt myself choking up as I looked at the photo. It was taken outside the Salt Lake City Temple. What caught my attention was, first of all, how beautiful my mom was, and second, how happy they both looked. Especially my dad. I don't think I'd ever seen him look that happy before.

Norton reminded me we had to go.

"Let us give you a ride," my grandfather said.

"No, we'll be fine. We'll be on the train for just a few minutes, and then a quick walk to the bus station."

We thanked them again, and I hugged them both before Norton and I stepped out the front door. They came out on the porch to watch us go.

"Don't forget us, Adam," my grandmother called out. "We have always loved you, and we will always love you."

"I love you both. I'll come back some day."

"You'd better."

We waved and hurried down the street toward the train station.

Two hours later I boarded a bus to my new area.

3

March came in like a lion, and the lion had a name. Elder Russell, a former Marine, was my new companion. He was also the district leader. He had a square jaw, a muscular frame, a military-style haircut, and a hoarse, deafening voice that he'd developed shouting commands to the troops.

Because Russell and I had come out about the same time, I thought we'd be equal partners. But those hopes were dashed shortly after Russell picked me up at the bus station. "If you're willing to work hard and obey mission rules, then you and I shouldn't have any problems."

"I always obey mission rules."

Russell shook his head. "That's not what I've heard, but let me say this, you will obey the rules with me. We can do this the easy way, or we can do this the hard way. It's totally up to you."

I resented being labeled a problem elder. With the exception of visiting my grandparents, I had always done my best to obey mission rules. But now, because of Doneau freaking

42

out and complaining to the president, there wasn't much I could do. Twenty-two months into my mission, and I had been demoted to junior companion.

In fact, Russell treated me like I'd just come out. For me this was both humiliating and depressing. The hardest thing was to come up with something positive to say in my letters home. I didn't want to let on how miserable I was.

Russell was a take-charge kind of guy. He taught every discussion. He did every door approach. Every success we had was Russell's.

That was bad enough, but when zone conference came, Russell bragged about each success and turned it into an example for the other missionaries to follow. He made himself look good, while I sat there quietly with my head lowered, counting the days until I would be released.

It seemed so unfair to me because, even when I was growing up, I'd never given my folks or my church leaders any reason to worry about me. I'd always tried to live the way I'd been taught. And now here I was, through no fault of my own, being treated like a complete slacker.

What had I done wrong? Nothing. Oh, well, okay, I called her *dear* once, but anybody listening would have known I was being sarcastic. Was that reason enough to send me to mission boot camp, with Russell as my drill sergeant?

Because Russell didn't need me for anything except to tag along with him, I soon found myself becoming detached from the work. Every morning, while Russell took a shower, I studied the photo of my dad and my real mom taken on their wedding day, standing in front of the Salt Lake City Temple.

They were not much older than me when the picture was taken. Each time I looked at it, I was struck by how beautiful my mom was and how happy my dad looked.

I'd heard enough stories already about how spontaneous and fun she was to be with. She was not at all like my stepmother. Lara was always serious and focused. I couldn't imagine her ever doing anything crazy or irresponsible.

I wrote each week to my New Jersey grandparents, encouraging them to continue studying with the sisters. In their letters to me, they kept me up-to-date on what they had learned about the Church. They also, at my request, told me more about my real mom—details about when she was growing up and more about my parents' courtship and things they did in the few years they were married.

I also got a letter once a week from my Utah mom. My dad didn't write much. He told my mom whatever he wanted to say to me, and she passed it on.

As the days dragged on, I became more miserable and even more resentful toward Sister Doneau for ruining my mission.

On Saturday, March 16, my grandparents called me at nine at night. "Well, we did it, Adam, we got baptized!" my grandfather said.

"That is so great! Congratulations!"

"Who are you talking to?" Russell asked.

"My grandparents. They just got baptized."

"You're only authorized to talk to family on Mother's Day and Christmas."

I ignored him while first my grandfather and then my grandmother told me every detail of their baptism.

"We have someone else who wants to talk to you," my grandfather announced.

After a brief pause, Doneau said, "Hello, Elder Roberts. It was a wonderful baptism. Everyone felt the Spirit."

I tried to be gracious. "I'm sure they did. Thank you for doing such a great job teaching."

"It's been the highlight of my mission."

"I can see why it would be."

"Wait a minute," Russell said. "You just thanked somebody

for teaching. Are you talking to Sister Doneau? She's the one you fell for, isn't she?"

"I didn't fall for her."

"You are talking to her, though, aren't you?" he demanded.

"Yeah, just for a minute, though."

"You got no business talking to her."

"Five minutes, Elder, five minutes. That's all I need," I said.

"I'm letting the president know about this."

"Yes, I'm sure you will. I'll be on the phone another five minutes."

He went to get his watch to time me.

When Doneau and I first started talking, I could hear my grandparents in the background, but now those background sounds were gone. "Where are you now?" I asked.

"I'm in the backyard," Sister Doneau said. "There's something you should know. I told you I phoned President McNamara before you were transferred, but I didn't tell you what I said to him about us. In all honesty, I think I need to tell you."

"Us? There is no *us*, Sister Doneau. There never was. There never will be."

"I had a dream. In my dream you and I were at the courthouse to get a marriage license. We got into an argument about whether I was going to take your name or you were going to take my name. It seemed so real. Anyway, the next day, I got scared and called President McNamara."

I was so mad I could barely talk. "Let me get this straight. Because you had some stupid dream, you blabbed to the president and got me transferred? I can't believe it! I should be where you are right now. I should be celebrating my grandparents' baptism. Instead of that, I'm here with Elder Drill Sergeant for a companion! Thanks a lot, Doneau! Good-bye and good luck! I really hope I never see you again!"

I slammed the phone down.

Of course Russell reported me to the president, who told him to keep his eye on me.

I didn't think it was possible, but after that, Russell became even more of a pain than before, but, even so, some good came from it. I had to give up the hope I'd had of stringing together a series of successes I could brag about when I reported my mission to my home ward.

All my life I had been encouraged to achieve, to get good grades, to improve my talents, and to make something of myself. My mom made me take piano lessons from third grade until when I rebelled at age sixteen. She was the reason I got my Eagle rank in Scouting.

But there's a price you pay for focusing your attention on achievements. That price was, for me, losing sight of why I did the things I did.

On a mission, when most of the missionaries think you're a problem elder, you're not going to get much praise for any success you have. So you either quit, develop a bad attitude, or else you start to think about the real reason why you're serving a mission.

I began to think about Who it was I was representing as a missionary. A missionary represents the Savior. Once I recognized that, I didn't worry anymore about the petty annoyance of being with Russell.

It's not easy to do that. It takes a lot of concentration. And it takes not caring who gets the credit.

My prayers became more Christ-centered. I looked at people differently than before. Instead of thinking of them as potential baptisms, I began to think of them as my brothers and sisters, each of us a child of our Father in Heaven.

Good came from my change in attitude because during April, my last month in the mission field, Russell and I had two baptisms. Of course Russell bragged about it in our next zone conference, and he didn't mention any part I might have played. I didn't mind though. He had his reward, and I had mine.

My time with Elder Russell had given me a chance to think about my life. This is what I came up with:

1. I don't want to spend my life going after goals that don't matter and aren't even mine, no matter how impressive they are.

2. I now knew that Heavenly Father can bless us even when we're not in a race to impress others. He is pleased when we try to love and serve others, especially if we're not doing it to gratify our own pride.

3. And, finally, I now could imagine that I would have probably turned out much different if my real mom hadn't died. I think I would have been a much more upbeat person, and definitely more fun to be with.

◆   ◆   ◆

Doneau left the mission in early April. I was to be released the last week in April.

I asked permission to visit my grandparents before I left the mission field, but that request was denied. "Just follow the mission rules, Elder," President McNamara said.

A few days before my mission was over, I called my grandparents and told them I wouldn't be able to visit them.

They were disappointed but said they understood.

On my last day, I met with President McNamara. He gave me a great deal of counsel. I could see he still thought of me as a problem missionary, but instead of letting that upset me, I felt a kind of peace. I knew I had tried and felt as though the Savior knew my heart.

And then the mission assistants drove me to the Newark Airport. Just before entering the security check, I spotted Eddie and Claire.

"Oh, my gosh!" I shouted, running to greet them. I hugged

my grandmother first and then my grandfather. "This is such a surprise! I didn't expect to see you here!"

"You think we'd let you sneak out of here without saying good-bye?" my grandfather called out. "We brought you some going away gifts!"

"What are they?"

My grandmother handed me a plastic container. "This is cannoli. You can eat it on the plane or now. Whatever you like."

"If I tried to eat it on the plane, there'd be a mutiny because the other passengers weren't getting any. So in the interests of safety, I'll eat it now. That way, even if the plane crashes, I'll be happy."

They didn't laugh much about the plane crashing. "Your plane isn't going to crash," my grandfather said. "We've prayed about it too much for that to happen." He handed me a box.

"What's this?"

"The caboose for your train set. I'll send the rest of the set later."

"Great. Thanks. I'll make good use of it at home."

He looked puzzled. "How?"

"I'll run a branch line into the kitchen and instruct my mom anytime the train shows up she's to fill it with food and send it back."

"You'll do no such thing," my grandmother scolded, "but if anyone were to cater to your every whim, it would be Lara. She's been such a good mom to you."

We sat down while I finished off the dessert. "This is even better than I remembered it."

"I'm glad you like it," my grandmother said.

I looked at my watch. "I'd better get going."

"When will we see you again?" my grandfather asked.

"I'll come visit you before school starts in the fall," I said, standing up and giving them each a hug before I started on my way.

"You'd better."

"I will. I promise."

"We love you," my grandmother called out.

"I love you too."

I waved at them and got in line to go through security.

An hour later, from the window seat of my plane, I caught one last look as a missionary at the New Jersey coastline.

All the way home, I couldn't decide if I was going home—or leaving home.

4

Ten minutes before the sacrament meeting started in which I was to report my mission, I shook hands with the bishopric and sat down on the stand, saving the seat next to the first counselor for the youth speaker.

My mom and dad and their parents, and some uncles and aunts and a couple of my cousins filled up the first few rows at the front of the chapel. My dad, his dark hair splattered with gray, wearing a dark brown suit with brown tie, looked like your typical member of the stake high council, which he was.

My mom looked very impressive too. She'd always been trim, and still was, but after I got home from my mission she reluctantly admitted that she now had to go to aerobics three times a week to maintain her weight.

My mom, whose maiden name had been Whyte, grew up on a farm near Idaho Falls, and so I spent part of each summer on the farm, working for my Grandfather Whyte. He was tall and strong, a simple man with a rural twang in his deep voice. He didn't say much, but what he said was worthwhile.

My Grandmother Whyte was still a powerhouse of energy and good health, and she attributed it all to homeopathic remedies. As a child, I learned quickly never to admit being sick in her presence because she had an herb for every complaint. Her other main characteristic was a love of learning. It was from her that my mom had learned to value education.

My grandparents on the Roberts side were also there. I remembered when I was a boy, how happy they were to cater to my every wish. It was always fun staying at their house. They gave me almost anything I asked for. If I wanted cake, my grandmother would bake it. If I wanted a toy, my grandfather would buy it. My mom once asked them if they ever said no to me. They paused, smiled, and said, "Why of course not. Why would we do that?"

After two years of being away, I could see more clearly that all four of my grandparents were getting older. They walked a little slower, spent a little more time getting things done, but they kept going.

In addition to my family, there were also a few friends from high school at the meeting; some of them had also just returned from their missions.

I looked at what few notes I had written on a three-by-five card. For three days I had tried to prepare a talk but had never decided for sure what to say. I couldn't bring myself to brag about any success I might have had because I hated the way Elder Russell had boasted at zone conferences, taking all the glory for himself, sometimes even forgetting to acknowledge Heavenly Father's help.

Since I didn't want to talk about either my successes or my failures, there wasn't much left.

A twelve- or thirteen-year-old girl came and sat next to me. She had long blonde hair and blue eyes and was energetically chewing gum.

"You giving a talk, too?" I asked.

She rolled her eyes. "Duh."

"What's your name?"

"Kierra. We moved next door to you just before you left on your mission."

"Sorry, I didn't recognize you. Well, that's nice, Kara."

She shook her head. "It's not Kara. It's not Karen. It's not Tara. It's not Carolyn. It's *Key*, like a key you open a door with, and then, *air*, like the air you breathe, and then, *ah*, like when a doctor looks in your mouth. Put them together and what have you got?"

I figured that Sister Doneau, as a girl, must have once been exactly like her. "I have no idea," I said.

She gave a pained sigh and rolled her eyes. "Okay, I'll do it one more time. Listen up, okay? It's *Key*, like a key you open a door with, *air*, like the air you breathe, and *ah*, like when a doctor looks in your mouth. Put them together and what have you got?"

I was in no mood for this girl. "A pain in the butt?"

Kierra's mouth dropped open. She turned to the first counselor in the bishopric. "Brother Robinson, he just called me a pain in the butt."

The first counselor, a stern, no-nonsense, bald junior high school principal, glared at me.

"I was just kidding," I said, forcing a chuckle.

"Someone who's just come back from a mission shouldn't be going around talking like that," Kierra said.

To get myself off the hook, I tried to apologize. "You're absolutely right, Kierra. What I said was totally wrong, and I'm very sorry."

It wasn't enough. She leaned over to get the bishop's attention. "Bishop, he called me a pain in the butt, and he's a returned missionary."

The bishop looked at me and shook his head. "Why don't we all try to get in the right spirit for our sacrament meeting," he said.

"But he called me a—"

"The bishop wants us to be quiet now," I scolded her. "So take the gum out of your mouth and quit talking."

She scowled at me. "You're not my boss." She did take the gum out of her mouth though, wrapped it in a tissue, and put it in her scripture case. She then looked over her talk. It was two pages long and typed. I glanced over it. It wasn't that bad. Actually, I wished I had her talk.

"You seem really well-prepared for your talk," I said.

She nodded. "My sister helped me. Her name is Sierra."

"Let me guess. Think of a *sea*, think of *air*, and then, *ah*, like when a doctor looks in your mouth, right?"

She shushed me. "We're supposed to be quiet now, so we can get ready for sacrament meeting."

"How long is your talk?" I asked.

"Five minutes. I timed it."

"Can you make it longer?"

"Why would I want to do that?" she asked.

"My talk isn't very long." I showed her my three-by-five card.

She read out loud what was on the card. "'My talk . . . Mission . . . New Jersey.'"

She stared at me. "That's it? That's your whole talk? You should've had my sister help you. She's a junior, and she's very smart. She's over there."

She pointed to a spectacular-looking girl, who, like Kierra, had long blonde hair and blue eyes. I was happy to know that Sierra was a junior. That would make her the same age as me. I wondered if she was going to BYU, where I'd be in the fall.

Trying to communicate to her older sister, Kierra pointed at me and mouthed the words about what I'd called her. Apparently Sierra didn't read lips because she just smiled.

It was a huge relief when sacrament meeting began.

After the sacrament was over, while the choir sang, I worried about what Kierra might say about me in her talk. "You don't need to tell everyone in your talk about what I said to you, okay?"

"I'll say whatever I want to say."

"Please don't ruin this for my family," I pleaded. "Everyone's here, my mom, my dad, my grandparents . . ."

"You should've thought about that before you swore at me."

"I didn't swear at you, Kierra."

A short time later Kierra got up to speak. "This morning when I sat down, Adam Roberts, who just got off his mission, called me a pain in the butt."

Everyone laughed, which was not the reaction she wanted. And so to drive her point home, she turned and glared at me. "You're not setting a very good example, you know, especially for a returned missionary. If this is how you act in church, then what are you like the rest of the time? You know what? I don't think you were a very good mission-ary." She then turned to face the congregation. "I will now give my talk."

I avoided eye contact with my parents, especially my mom. She liked things to be done a certain way, and this wasn't the way. I didn't think my dad would mind as much. He never did. My mother was always the one who was upset about the small things that I would do that she thought were either wrong or inappropriate.

Exactly five minutes and forty seconds later, Kierra sat down. It was my turn. I had thirty minutes.

I stood up and began. "I just got back from serving a mission to the New Jersey Morristown Mission." I paused. "I learned a great deal from my mission."

At that point panic set in.

In the congregation Sierra, the older sister, was looking at me, but as the silence continued, out of politeness, she dropped her gaze and opened her scriptures. My parents and grandparents were all smiling nervously, willing me to go on.

Behind me on the stand, Kierra tried in her own way to help me. "Don't just stand there. Tell 'em what you learned on your mission!"

Nothing came to mind.

"Say something!" Kierra demanded.

"On my mission I learned that . . ." I sighed, " . . . that if the only reason you're on a mission is to impress your family, and you want to end up as a district leader or a zone leader so your family will be proud, then you're not there for the right reason. The best thing is to just do your best in whatever situation you're put in, no matter how hard it is. Like if you have a bad companion for example. No matter what, your job as a missionary is to . . ."

I quit talking, not because I didn't have anything to say, but because what I wanted to say was too close to my heart, and I needed to try to say it without getting too emotional.

A tear slid down my cheek. I had always been embarrassed for guys who lose it while giving a talk in church. Now I was one of them.

I wiped my cheek. "I want to talk to the young men in the ward about when you go on your mission. Your calling as a missionary is to represent the Savior to everyone you talk to. If you focus on that, then nothing else matters because every conversation you have, with every person you meet, is really important.

"I never held a leadership position on my mission, and I didn't have that many baptisms, and my last few months were tough, but none of that matters now. What matters is that I know that Jesus Christ is our Savior and Redeemer, and He loves every person. That's what I learned."

I cleared my throat. "On my mission I had a chance to teach my grandparents the gospel. You might not know this, but my dad, when he was about my age, married a girl from back East. Her name was Charlene, but everybody called her Charly. Her dad was transferred out here by his company, and she was a convert to the Church. She died when I was about a year old, and sometime after that, her folks moved back to New Jersey. I was able to look them up and got a chance to teach them the missionary lessons. After I was transferred, they were baptized. Getting to know them and having them become members of the Church was one of the best experiences of my mission.

"I also got a chance to learn more about my mom . . . my real mom. I don't know how to say this because, the truth is, the only mom I've ever known is sitting right there." I pointed to Lara. "But the one who gave me life, well, I got to know more about her from my New Jersey grandparents. I found out that she was really wonderful. So learning about her was good. And I came to really love my other grandparents as much as I love the ones who are here today."

I chuckled. "One thing I found out that I'd never known before is that my dad, before he married my real mom, got arrested in New York City for disturbing the peace. Can you believe that about my dad? I guess what happened was my dad and, well, Charly is what they called her, they had an argument when she was living here, and she got so mad at him she went back East. So my dad went out there and tried to patch things up. And I guess he must have flipped out or something. He was so crazy about this girl."

My mom's face was frozen into a polite smile.

"Anyway, my dad got arrested. They told him they'd let him go if he promised never to come back. So I was thinking— maybe his name and picture are on the wall of some police station even to this day."

A couple of people laughed, but my mom closed her eyes and lowered her head. Dad was just staring at me without any expression.

"But you know, it's okay. I can understand how something like that could happen. I mean, after all, he was really in love

56

so . . ." I chuckled again. "It's just really weird to me to think of my dad being handcuffed and taken away by the police."

I could see people starting to squirm a bit, and it got very quiet in the chapel. That's when it occurred to me that I was maybe making my talk just a little too interesting. I decided I didn't want to talk anymore about my mission, so I read three or four scriptures that had come to mean a great deal to me, bore my testimony, and sat down.

We got out of sacrament meeting early, which made everyone happy. Right after the meeting ended, Kierra hurried over to talk to her older sister, who gave her a hug. I couldn't hear what Kierra was telling her, but it was easy to imagine. I guessed the little brat was describing in great detail how messed up I was.

My family and I went home for dinner. Sometimes it's hard to tell if my mom is mad or just very busy. This was one of those times.

"Mom, can I help you do anything?" I asked, even though both my grandmothers were already working beside her.

"I think we have things pretty much in control, Adam, but if you want to do something, how about filling up the water glasses?"

"Sure, I can do that." I went to the cupboard and got a pitcher and filled it with water.

She caught me looking at her and knew what it meant. "I'm not upset with you, Adam."

"I guess I shouldn't have told 'em about Dad being picked up in New York."

"It wouldn't have been what I'd have said in a sacrament meeting talk, but I'm sure we'll survive . . ," she broke into a grin, " . . . the scandal of it all."

I felt more relaxed that she could smile about it, and went about filling the water glasses in the dining room.

My grandparents didn't say much about my talk, which wasn't a good sign.

A few minutes later we were ready to sit down and eat. My mom had set an honorary place for Quentin, who was on his mission. Just before we had a blessing on the food, she read part of a letter from Quentin. Apparently his mission president was amazed at how quickly he was picking up the language. "They say Finnish is probably the most difficult foreign language to learn," my mom told us.

"Well, the fact he's brilliant doesn't surprise me," my grandfather on my mom's side said. "Look at the genes he's got."

I smiled faintly, trying my best not to look hurt. Quentin's genes were different from my genes because we had different mothers.

"That's true," I agreed. "Quentin is very smart. I'm sure he's an outstanding missionary."

After my dad said the blessing, and we started to fill our plates, my grandfather on my dad's side asked, "What are you going to do this summer, Adam?"

"Ah . . . well . . . I'm not sure. I haven't really thought about it."

"You'll be working for us, won't you?" my mom asked.

"I don't know. Like I said, I really haven't thought about it."

"Well, we just assumed you'd come back to work with us again," my mom said.

"I probably will. I just haven't thought about it."

"We have a family business and we need family support," my mom said. "Quentin helped out when you were on your mission, now it's your turn to help him. At least that's the way I see it."

"Let me take some time this week to look for a job, and if I don't find anything, then I'll work for you guys."

"We'd love to have you, but we'll support whatever decision you make," my dad said.

"Thanks," I said.

58

"Are you excited to go to BYU in the fall?" my mom asked.

"Yeah, I am."

"Have you looked at the classes I signed you up for?"

"No, I haven't."

"You can still make changes if you want. But, of course, the freshman year is pretty much laid out."

I paused, not knowing if I should admit that I wasn't sure I wanted to major in information systems. Of course it made the most sense, in terms of my dad's company, but even so, I wanted some time to think about other possible careers.

For years my dad has had a business that sets up Web sites for small companies that might not see a need for a Web site. He's been the only salesman, so he was on the road a lot. Quentin and I had always stayed in the office, cranking out Web sites, mostly for one-person companies. My mom was the office manager, which hadn't always been the best for our mother-son relationship because, at work, she demanded perfection.

Here's the kind of small businesses we serve: On a fly-fishing trip to Strawberry Reservoir when I was in high school, my dad stopped at a bait shop in Heber City to buy some flies. While there, he talked the owner into getting a Web site, and now this man sells his hand-tied flies to fishermen around the world.

Since we've mainly catered to small businesses, what we were doing was below the radar screen for other Web site companies, so we filled a niche without fear of being made obsolete. When the economy was good, our business was great, but even when the economy was bad, and people were getting laid off, some would start up their own company. And as we could find them, they signed on too.

I had worked for my dad since I was in ninth grade—after school for a couple of hours and full-time during the summer. My job was to sit in front of a computer and churn out Web sites, answering questions from computer novices about mostly simple things that any fifteen-year-old would know.

Before I left on my mission I had gotten very good at designing Web sites. And Quentin was right behind me. But with him gone, Mom and Dad didn't have anyone to do the technical stuff. That's why they were so anxious for me to get home and come back to work.

My mom had made my favorite dessert for the occasion. Chocolate cake. She cut me the first piece and, after setting it in front of me, kissed me on the cheek, and said, "Welcome home, Adam."

"Thanks, Mom."

After we finished eating, we all went into the living room to talk.

As we were finding seats, my mom said, "It's such a small world. You know that Elder Russell you worked with?"

Sergeant Russell was, of course, my last companion—or as I used to think of him, my last warden.

"Sure. What about him?"

"I guess he's writing a girl in our stake. Her name is Melissa Hutton. I ran into her mother at the store the other day, and she told me he had written Melissa to say you were companions."

"Really? What did he say?"

"I don't know, but her mother said Melissa knew all about you."

Knowing what Russell would write about me, I had a sinking feeling that before long my mom would be told by the mother of Russell's girlfriend that I'd been a slacker on my mission, and that I'd tried to romance a sister missionary.

"There are so many cute girls who are just dying to spend time with you," my mom went on.

"Really? Who?"

"Oh, girls in the ward, who have grown up since you've been gone, and some others in the stake. I know a lot of them have been anxious for you to get home. Didn't you notice how many were in sacrament meeting today?"

"Sounds like you're going to be busy, Adam," Grandpa Whyte said, giving me a big wink.

I didn't want to talk about girls or Elder Russell, so I decided to draw my dad out. "Dad, how's the business going?"

He smiled. "It's going very well. You remember Bait Man Bob in Heber? You set up his Web site before your mission."

"Right."

"Well, we're expanding that now. We're going to set up one site that will bring together all the best fly tyers in the world. I'll be flying out Thursday to an international fly-tying convention. I hope to get as many people as I can to sign on to a part of this Web site. So if this goes through, you're going to have plenty of work to do."

"That sounds great, Dad."

After my grandparents left, my mom asked if she could speak with me.

"Sure. What's up?"

"Let's go outside."

She gave me a tour of the garden and asked me if I could do some weeding and rake up the dead leaves from under our bushes in the next few days.

"No problem."

Then she said, "There's something else."

"Okay."

"I'm glad you got to meet your mother's . . . Charly's parents. How was it? I mean, getting to know them? Did they tell you a lot about her?"

Lara and I had hardly ever talked about my birthmother. I had been so young when Charly died, and Lara had been the only mother I had ever known. But from what Claire and Eddie had told me, I knew Lara had been sensitive about her role as a "replacement" mom. Something told me I needed to be careful about what I might say.

"Yeah, they did."

"I never met her, of course. Your father and I met after . . . after she had died. But apparently she was one of those people who everyone loves."

"That's what her parents said."

I wanted to ask something, but wasn't sure how my mom would take it. After hesitating, I said, "Why haven't you and Dad told me more about her?"

She shook her head. "Maybe we should have. I just felt that, well, I'm your mom, and I didn't want to confuse you."

I nodded. "That makes sense."

She gave me a sad little smile then drew me into a hug. "I don't mind if you think about her . . . as long as you also remember how much I love you."

"Okay, I'll do that."

◆　　◆　　◆

On Monday I tried to find a job but didn't run into anything I really wanted to do.

After a couple of hours, I quit looking and went home. I grabbed some cookies and took a swig of milk right out of the carton from the fridge. I knew it was something that drove my mom crazy, but hey, old habits die hard. Then I changed clothes and went out to do some yard work.

I was raking up dead leaves when someone called out, "Hi!"

It was Sierra, Kierra's older sister from next door. She was standing on her patio, waving and smiling.

"Hi, yourself," I said.

She walked toward the low fence between our yards. "Great talk yesterday!" she said with a teasing grin, showing off some very white teeth and confirming she was as good-looking as I had thought when I saw her from the stand. "I didn't even fall asleep."

"Are you here so I can apologize for what I said about Kierra? I can do it. In fact, bring your whole family over. I'd be happy to apologize to each and every one, together or one at a time. I can also grovel too. Hey, whatever you guys want."

She laughed. "Look, don't worry about it. I'm on your side. Kierra can be a pain in the butt. So you were right about that."

"You can say that here when she's not around. Try saying it sitting next to her sometime just before sacrament meeting is about to begin. That separates the men from the boys."

She laughed. "Which of those two are you?"

I gave her a weak smile. "Very good. Pour it on. Show no mercy."

"Don't be so self-conscious, okay? Everyone in the ward understands why you'd say what you said about Kierra."

"So, if you didn't come to get an apology, why are you here?"

"I'm supposed to cut the lawn, but I can't get the mower started. Can you help me?"

I went over to her place and tried several times to get her mower started but couldn't do it, so I went ahead and cut her lawn with our mower.

As I was finishing up, she brought me out some lemonade, and we sat on her patio to drink it. "That was so nice of you. Now let me help you. What would you have been doing instead of mowing our lawn?"

"Raking up leaves."

"I'll help you then," she offered.

"You don't have to."

"I want to."

"Why?"

"Just for fun." She looked at me and smiled. She had a very winning smile.

I raked while she stuffed the leaves into bags.

"So, tell me more about your mission."

"There isn't much to tell, except I ended my mission with everyone thinking I wasn't a very good missionary."

"How come?"

I told her about my grandparents, and about Doneau getting me transferred.

"She got you transferred because she had a dream about you? That's not fair."

"It doesn't matter now. I'm over it."

She laughed. "I can tell."

"When I got transferred, my new companion was told I was a problem elder, so he treated me like his prisoner. He never gave me a chance to do anything. I was the designated junior companion. I just followed him around."

"You poor guy. That must have been so hard for you."

"It was."

She put her hand on my arm. "Sometimes when things aren't going the way we'd like, that's the biggest test we ever face. I'm proud of you for not giving up."

I looked at her. Her eyes really were a great shade of blue. "You know what? I can't remember the last time anyone said they were proud of me."

"Well, I guess I need to spend more time with you. You're smart, you're a nice guy, and you go out of your way to help someone in need, like I was when I couldn't start the mower." She paused. "And you're not too bad looking either."

I couldn't help but think this might have possibilities for the future.

"You're a junior, right? Do you go to BYU? I'll be there in the fall."

She hesitated for a second and then said, "My dad works for the University of Utah, so where do you think I go to school?"

"Makes sense."

"What will you be doing this summer?" she asked.

"I guess I'll work for my dad."

She invited me to have lunch with her at her place. We talked while she made sandwiches, then we ate on her patio.

After we finished, I stood up and said, "I'd better go. Thanks for a great day."

"It was a great day for me too."

She came very close and looked up at me. "You want to do something tonight?" she asked.

"Yeah, sure, that'd be great."

"This is for being such a help to me today." She gave me a hug. It was just her way of showing appreciation. Unfortunately, though, it occurred just as Kierra got home. She saw us through the kitchen window, then opened the sliding door and came outside.

"All right, what's going on?"

"Nothing," Sierra said, smiling.

"That's not true. You two were hugging!"

"I was just thanking him for mowing the lawn," Sierra said, holding my arm.

"You shouldn't be hugging my sister."

"I didn't hug her. She hugged me."

"You were hugging back. And that's not right because she's still in high school. You're way too old for her."

My mouth dropped open. "You're still in high school?" I asked Sierra.

"I'll be a junior."

"In high school?"

"Yes, but I'm very mature for my age."

"You told me you were a junior at the University of Utah."

"I didn't exactly say that." She paused. "But, I guess I did want you to think I was in college."

"Why would you do that?"

"Because you'd never even want to talk to me if you knew

I was in high school. I'm tired of high school guys. They're so immature."

"Maybe you can help them become more responsible."

She shook her head. "Look, I don't want much from you. Maybe if we could just talk once in a while, that's all."

"What would we talk about?"

"I don't know. Whatever you want."

Kierra shook her head. "I don't think you should spend time with someone who goes around saying I'm a pain in the butt."

Sierra scowled at her. "That's what you're being now," Sierra said.

"Sorry, guys. Hey, I know, let's shoot baskets," Kierra suggested.

And that's what we did. We played H.O.R.S.E. until suppertime. To be perfectly honest, it was the most fun I'd had since leaving for my mission. Even Kierra warmed up to me.

Later that night, right after we finished eating dinner, my mom asked me to tell her about Sister Doneau. That's when I knew the mother of the girl who was writing to Elder Russell had talked to my mom.

That explanation took me an hour. My mom and dad believed my version of what had happened between Doneau and me. They even said they felt sorry they hadn't known what a difficult time I'd been having the last few months of my mission.

By the time we were done talking, I felt like I'd given my parents enough cause for concern since coming home. I didn't want to cause any more problems, so I decided to give in. "Oh, another thing, I've decided to work for you guys this summer."

My mom burst into a big smile and kissed me on the cheek. "That's great, Adam! Not just because we'll be able to work together again, but also because it's so hard to find anyone as good and as fast as you are. Besides, I don't think you can earn better money than what we're going to pay you."

In his formal way, my dad shook my hand. Then we had family prayer and went to bed.

But I couldn't sleep. Having been away for two years, I felt like I was seeing my family in a new light. It was very clear to me how important my mom was to our family. Most of what I'd been able to accomplish in high school in terms of grades or music or even earlier in Scouting was because of my mom. That is, Lara.

In the past I'd never thought much about her not being my real mother because she was the only mom I'd ever known. But now, after learning a little about my birthmother, the one everyone called Charly, I had started to wonder what might have happened if my real mom hadn't died. How would I be different? Or, another way of asking the same question— was the tension I felt between Lara and me due to our not really being connected by blood? I mean, maybe I got my basic personality from Charly, and Lara had always tried to make me conform to her way of thinking and doing things. What if all the time I was growing up, I was trying to fit into the pattern Lara had chosen for me, but deep inside, I was a completely different person?

What if I'm more like my real mom? I thought. It was a question that, at that point, I couldn't really answer, but one I couldn't help asking.

I knew that my dad could tell me more about what my real mom was like, but I didn't feel comfortable asking him. It might seem to him that I didn't appreciate the only mom I'd ever known.

Don't get me wrong. I loved Lara. She had always cared for me and loved me. It would be hard to imagine what my life would be like without her.

But this wasn't about her. It was more about me, and the haunting feeling that maybe I had never been true to who I really was. It's a bad analogy, but it was kind of like a hawk that had been raised by a family of ducks. There would come a time when he would discover that no matter how hard he tried to swim in the pond, it wasn't who he was—he wasn't a duck but something entirely different. That night was when I first began thinking of the only mother I'd ever known as "Lara." Lara wasn't my real mom. She wasn't the woman whose genes I carried.

My real mom's name is Charly, I thought just before falling asleep.

5

Two days later, the first Wednesday in May, I began working for my parents, designing Web sites as well as providing tech support. My dad was on the road most of the time, so my mom and I were together in the office all day. Sometimes it was hard to tell when she was being my mom and when she was being my supervisor. For example, on Friday of my first week, she sat down next to me. "Adam, we need to talk."

"Okay."

"I know you're just getting into this after two years, but I've noticed a trend I think we need to discuss."

Whenever Lara said, "There's something we need to *discuss*," it really meant, "I've thought about it, and you need to do something differently."

"What is it?" I asked.

"You do your work very fast. Much faster than even Quentin. So, that's good."

"I'm sure with a little practice I can get even faster."

She put her hand on my arm. "Well, actually, I don't need

you to get faster. In fact, I'd like you to slow down. You need to make sure you've done everything that needs to be done. I've made a checklist, and I'd like you to use it each time you work on a Web site." She handed me the checklist.

I looked it over. "Okay, sure, I can do that."

"I just think you'll be happier if you don't have to keep going back over what you've already done. Do it right the first time, even if it does take you more time."

It was, of course, a reasonable thing to ask. And I did do better once I began using the checklist, but it also felt like I was being hovered over.

It had always been like that. In grade school, my mom, that is, Lara, always checked my homework before I went to school. In junior high she mapped out what merit badges I needed in Scouts to get my Eagle. She had even helped me fill out my mission papers. And now, at age twenty-one, I was still being managed by her. I acted like I didn't resent it, but I did, and it gave me another excuse to unfairly compare Lara to my free-spirited, fun-loving real mom.

The truth is I didn't take much satisfaction from my job. I mean, what did I accomplish? Nothing you could touch, drive, cook on, camp in, or fish with. I envied the people we serviced—Bait Man Bob, the man in Heber who ties flies, or the woman in St. George who makes fancy quilts, or the woman in Indianapolis who bakes Greek pastries in her kitchen and ships them around the world to her customers. At least they produce something you can hold in your hand.

At home, when I went into the kitchen for a snack, Lara asked me for a hug. "I love you, Adam. You know that, don't you?"

"Yeah, I do. I love you too, Mom."

"I'm sorry if I come down on you sometimes at work."

"It's okay. Sometimes I need it."

After work the next day I got a phone call. "Adam, is that

you?" It was Eddie, my grandfather from New Jersey. "How are you doing, my boy?"

"Doing great."

"I'm glad to hear it. We've been missing you. What have you been up to? Are you working there?"

I told him that I was working for my dad, and I guess he picked up on my lack of enthusiasm.

"You want to come out here and work for me? I've always got more work than I can handle."

"What kind of work?"

"Mowing lawns, weeding, fixing leaky faucets, routine maintenance. I could teach you everything you need to know."

"Well, that sounds good, but my folks need me. I'd better stay here."

"I understand. But you'll come and visit us before school starts, though, won't you?"

"I will, for sure, you can count on it."

After I hung up, I felt bad for turning him down. Doing maintenance sounded a lot more fun than what I was doing.

Our home is located high on the east bench of Salt Lake City. We are well enough off to live in a house precariously clinging to the steep hillside. Everyone in our ward seems to do well financially, although I'm not sure what anyone does. I imagined most of the men also spent their lives in front of a computer monitor—buying, selling, moving virtual money from one location to another.

My mom and I rode to work together. She always drove, so I felt like I was in junior high again, being chauffeured around from place to place.

I wanted to buy a car, but my folks suggested I wait until I'd saved up at least part of what I would need for my freshman year of college. Since that wasn't going to happen anytime soon, I bought a mountain bike instead.

Instead of eating dinner with my dad and Lara, I began riding every evening. After we got home from work, I would

71

change and ride up into the mountains to the top of a peak overlooking the city, where I would sit on a rock and watch the sun set over the mountains west of the Great Salt Lake.

There, all alone, with my T-shirt still sweaty and my face caked with salt from my sweat and dust from my ride, I felt at peace with myself.

Once, I stayed too long and had to go down the trail in the dark. After that, I began taking a flashlight with me. I would usually get back from my ride just before ten, eat leftovers from the fridge, take a shower, and go right to bed.

Lara was serving as stake Relief Society president, and she knew lots of women in our stake and their unmarried daughters, often returned missionaries or girls who had graduated from college and were now working. Over the next little while, Lara lined me up with some of those girls. She would offer to loan me her car and even wanted to give me some money to pay for the dates. I used her car but wouldn't take her money. It seemed too much like a bribe. Besides, the dates were mostly a disaster.

In the middle of May, Lara came into my room after I'd returned home from riding up in the hills and showed me a picture of a girl. "Isn't she adorable?"

"I suppose."

"The picture really doesn't do her justice. Oh, her name is Jennifer. She teaches second grade. She loves kids. Her hobbies are scrapbooking and sewing, and her mother tells me she's a very good cook."

"Good for her," I said with a hint of sarcasm in my voice. I could only wonder what this girl's mother was saying about me. Something like: "He's a returned missionary. He's going to BYU in the fall. He works for his dad." And then a long pause. "He's a very nice boy."

I pitied both Jennifer and me that our lives had come to this.

Lara is very persistent, and so, on Saturday, I went out with Jennifer.

Because our mothers had set us up, there was way too much riding on this. We both knew that when we got home, our mothers would be hoping we'd say, "I've met the love of my life. I'm sure this is the one!"

"You must be an excellent teacher," I said over salad at the Italian restaurant I had chosen.

She smiled. "Well, I don't know about that. But I do love the kids in my class."

"I love kids, too," I said. Long pause. But then I panicked. "Not that I want any of my own anytime soon." I wiped my brow.

After a painful lull in the conversation, I said, "You look nice tonight."

"Oh, thanks. You, too."

She was trying so hard to impress me that when she spilled her drink and some of it ran across the table and got my pants wet, she got all flustered. "I'm so sorry!"

"No, it's okay, really. Don't worry about it. I spill all the time." To ease her mind, I knocked over my water glass. "There you go. Now we're even."

She started laughing. "You can probably see I'm a little nervous tonight."

"Tell me about it. I feel like we're doing this for our mothers. I can imagine them on their knees right now, praying we'll hit it off."

She laughed. "*Are* we hitting it off?"

"Look, you've gone out on dates like this before, right?"

She nodded. "Dozens of times."

"And nothing's come from any of them, right?"

"Right."

"So most likely nothing will come from this. So just relax, okay? We'll eat. We'll talk. We'll go to a movie. We will have done our duty, then we'll go home. Nothing to it."

Her lower lip began to quiver. I felt awful. "Look, going out with me isn't exactly the chance of a lifetime. The truth is I'm not much of a catch. You can do a lot better."

"Really?" she asked, looking hopeful once again.

"Absolutely. In fact, one thing you should know, I was a problem elder on my mission." I said it as if it were something to brag about.

She looked puzzled. "Thank you for telling me, I guess."

"No problem. Glad to help out."

She seemed to relax a bit after that. She even asked if we could have dessert. Of course I said yes. I looked over the menu and recommended cannoli, so we both ordered it.

"So, you teach second grade, right? Let me ask you a question. When you have parent-teacher conferences, can you usually tell which parents go with which kid?"

"Sometimes."

"Because the kid looks like his folks, right?"

"Yes, most of the time that's true."

"Okay, but could you tell which mom went with which kid by the way the kid acts in class? I mean, like, if a mom is outgoing and friendly, would her son be like that too? Or if a mom is kind of a perfectionist, would her boy be like that?"

"Sometimes, but not always."

"Could we go to your classroom?"

"Sure. If you want to."

"I do. Finish up and let's go."

A few minutes later I got a tour of her classroom. She spent ten minutes showing me the calendar and posters and pictures she had made to hang on her classroom wall, and she showed me her lesson plans. She talked with great enthusiasm.

"You just light up when you talk about teaching," I said.

"I love it."

At my suggestion we sat down across from each other in the tiny desks.

"I wasn't a good student in grade school," I said. "I was smart enough, but I was easily distracted. I found the people in my class more interesting than the textbooks. I guess I'm still that way."

I talked about my childhood, and she listened politely and even asked me some questions.

An hour later I looked at my watch. "Oh, my gosh, we've missed our movie."

She shrugged. "I don't care."

"Me either, actually," I said, standing up. "Let's go. I've bored you enough for one night."

"Why did you tell me about when you were in grade school?"

"Well, the truth is, and I know this sounds lame, but I'm trying to find out who I am."

On the way home, she asked, "Were you really a problem elder on your mission?"

I thought about it, then said, "I don't know how to answer that. I worked hard and always tried to do my best. But I did get in hot water with my mission president."

"What did you do?"

"One of the sister missionaries thought I liked her. That wasn't true, but she called our mission president and complained, and he took her word and transferred me. After that I had a bad reputation."

A few minutes later we were standing on her porch. "If you told me now that you liked me, it wouldn't get you into trouble," she said.

"I do like you, Jennifer, but there's something you need to understand."

"What?"

"Until I get things figured out in my mind, I'm not going to be much good to you, or to anyone."

She gave me a sad little smile and then quickly kissed me

on the cheek. "Call me anytime you need someone to talk to." And then she went inside.

One thing was very clear to me as I drove home. I had no business seeing anyone until I got my life straightened out.

When I got home, I told Lara I would not let her line me up anymore.

"How are you going to meet other girls then?" she asked.

"I guess that's my problem, isn't it?"

"Why do you have to go biking every night after work?"

"I have to. It's the only way I can unwind."

I continued to withdraw into myself, and that led to another problem. On the last Thursday in May, after biking up the mountain and back, I ate, took a shower, then, instead of going to bed, I decided to get on my computer and check my e-mail.

I sat down at the computer in my room and started to surf the Web, and, within minutes, by not being careful, I ended up at a porn site. Instead of immediately getting out, I decided to see how bad it was. It was very bad, and when I turned off my computer an hour later, I vowed never to do that again.

But the next day, I couldn't quit thinking about what I had seen, and late that night, after Lara and Dad were in bed, I found myself sitting in front of my computer, feeling guilty but unable to turn away.

On Saturday night, I returned to the site again. I knew that what I was doing was wrong, and I felt guilty, and I once again promised myself I'd never go back.

On Sunday morning, as I got ready for church, the seriousness of what I'd done during the week hit me. I didn't feel like going to church, but I knew if I didn't, my mom and dad would want to know why. If I said I was sick, Lara wouldn't just let it go. She'd do everything she could to make sure I got better.

I decided to go to church because if I didn't it would raise too many red flags for my parents.

I thought I could just fake it, but once the meeting began, I knew I couldn't in good conscience partake of the sacrament, but if I didn't, my mom and dad would notice and they'd want to know why.

During the opening song, I turned to my dad. "I left something in the car I need to get."

I wandered into the cultural hall and looked around. The hall was dark, providing a dreary setting that perfectly matched my mood. I sat on the stage and waited for the sacrament to be blessed and passed.

I could hear the meeting through the sound system, and during the prayer on the bread, I sat with my shoulders slumped and my head down. Waves of guilt washed over me. I'd heard all the warnings about how destructive Internet pornography could be, and the images I'd viewed popped into my mind. It was driving me crazy. *I've got to stop this*, I thought. *If I don't, it will destroy me.*

When the sacrament was over, I went into the chapel and sat in the overflow area for the talks. After sacrament meeting, on my way to class, I ran into the bishop. He said hello and stopped to talk. I thought about asking to set up an appointment with him, but I decided I needed to get the problem under control before I met with him. He'd been my bishop since I was a priest. He'd always spoken highly of me. I didn't want to disappoint him.

Monday was Memorial Day. I began the day with optimism that I could overcome this problem. I worked with my folks in the yard during the day. At four we went over to my grandparents' on my dad's side for a barbecue. There was enough family around to take my mind off my problems.

That night at two-thirty in the morning, I woke up to go to the bathroom. When I returned, I turned on my computer and once again, messed up.

On Tuesday after work, when my folks and I pulled into our driveway, Sierra and Kierra were shooting baskets in their driveway. "Adam, get over here right now!" Kierra said, sounding like a drill sergeant.

When I was a few feet from them, she passed me the ball. "Go ahead and shoot! I dare you. You'll never make it!"

"Why do you say that?"

"Because I just know."

I shot and missed.

"No big surprise there," Kierra said, smiling at me. "Watch this." She shot from the same spot and missed.

"No big surprise there," I said with a slight smile.

"You want to play H.O.R.S.E.?" Kierra asked.

Sierra, the one closer to my age, wasn't saying much of anything, but when I passed the ball to her, she smiled at me.

"I'll take you both on," I said in my most menacing tone.

We had a great time. We pretended to care about the game, we traded insults, we laughed, we tried dumb trick shots, which we never made.

It was fun and I felt happy and glad for their friendship.

And then something happened. Sierra bent over to pick up the ball. Her shirt didn't cover everything and I saw skin. Nothing bad really. It wasn't what she did. It was what it made me think of.

Like a dam breaking, a flood of unworthy thoughts poured into my mind, and I was suddenly looking at these two innocent girls in a way that I had learned from watching pornography. They were no longer two cute girls who were fun to be with. I was looking at them as sexual objects, not girls with freckles, not girls who made me laugh, not nice, neighbor girls who were making an effort to be friends with me.

I must have thought I could keep the things I had seen on porn sites separate from the rest of my life. I didn't know it would not only alter how I looked at normal girls and women but how I felt about myself.

I felt dirty. I felt evil. I felt warped. I felt sick to my stomach.

I wanted to puke up the images I had stored in my mind by watching pornography.

I felt like I was carrying a disease within me, and the only way I could protect Sierra and Kierra was to leave. "I've got to go now," I muttered.

"But we haven't beat you yet!" Kierra called out.

I ran home, changed into my workout clothes, and rode away on my bike.

Half an hour later as I was biking up a trail, I kept asking myself *What have I done?*

I didn't want to sink deeper into the hole I was digging for myself. I wanted to stop watching pornography, but the truth was I wasn't sure I could. Not with a computer in my room, and not in a job where I worked on a computer every day.

At the top of the mountain, I cried, I prayed, I made resolutions, but at ten that night, while making my way slowly down the trail, I had doubts I would ever be able to stop.

It was a cloudy night—no stars, no moon—and my flashlight batteries were nearly dead. Halfway down the trail, the flashlight went out, and I was all alone in the dark. I could barely make out the trail ahead of me.

I stopped and knelt down and tried to pray, but it didn't work. I didn't feel worthy to pray. I thought I'd lost any chance that God would ever hear my prayers.

I quit praying and stood up. The darkness around me seemed to be enveloping me. Not only darkness but evil. Sick images from porn sites I'd visited flashed through my mind and wouldn't go away.

"No!" I shouted to the darkness.

I jumped on my bike and rode as fast as I could, recklessly defying the darkness, racing down the mountain in a headlong desperate flight from myself and from the depression that had closed in all around me.

More than anything, I wanted to escape the darkness

around me, and the darkness within me. I wanted to be bathed in light.

My front wheel hit a rock, and I went over the handlebars, hitting my head on a rock and knocking myself out.

I don't know how long I was unconscious, but when I came to, I sat up. My head was throbbing. I felt my forehead; it was bleeding.

I panicked, worrying I'd bleed to death. For the first time in my life, I was terrified of dying because I was not prepared to die.

I pleaded with God to spare my life, to give me one more chance, to help me turn my life around. I promised him if He would, I would never disappoint him again.

I'm not sure what I expected when I ended my prayer. What I hoped for was a way to get down the trail, but nothing had changed. If anything, the clouds were thicker, the visibility worse. Then it began to rain. I gave up any hope of making it down the trail.

I moved underneath a large pine tree and waited. Eventually my cut quit bleeding, and I went to sleep.

I woke up several times during the night. Each time I did, I thanked God that I was still alive and asked him to help me survive the night.

At four-thirty in the morning it stopped raining and started to get light enough to see my way down the trail.

My front wheel was bent, so I had to walk home, carrying my bike.

When I entered our house, I was relieved that my parents were still in bed. I guessed they'd fallen asleep before the time I usually came home. Otherwise, they would have been worried about me and been up trying to find out where I was.

I washed the wound on my forehead and the blood off my face. It looked like I might need stitches, but I was too tired to worry about that then. Instead, I went to bed and soon fell asleep.

A little before eight, my dad came into my room to wake me up. When I sat up, he saw my head.

"Adam? What happened?"

"I fell off my bike last night. I'm okay though."

"You've got to have a doctor examine you."

"I know. I'll go this morning."

"I'll take you."

"No, that's okay. You've got a plane to catch, don't you? I can get to the doctor."

"I'll take a later flight. Get dressed. I'm taking you."

My dad took me to our family doctor. The doctor examined me and cleaned the wound. He said it probably should have been stitched up, but that it was too late now. He cleaned it thoroughly and put a bandage on it.

When my dad and I left the doctor's office and got into the car, he turned to me and said, "Are you okay?"

"Yeah, sure. The doctor said—"

"I'm not talking about what the doctor said. Is something bothering you?"

"What about your travel plans?" I asked.

He shook his head. "It can wait."

I felt guilty for keeping my dad from his work. "Okay, look, you don't need to take the day off. I can tell you what the problem is now."

"Tell me then."

I turned away. I couldn't face him and say what I had to say. "It's pornography. I've been going online late at night."

"How long has this been a problem?"

I sighed. "It's been about a week. I've done it four times."

"What about before your mission?"

"Nothing before my mission. The first time I ever did anything like this was last Thursday. But it's taking over my life. After each time I promise myself I'm never going to do it again. But I keep messing up. Dad, I've got to stop this. No matter how much I say I'm not going to do it again, it still happens. I feel like I'm losing all my self-control."

He nodded. "Have you talked to the bishop?"

"I was hoping I could overcome the problem before I talked to him."

"You'll make faster progress with him than you will by yourself."

I shook my head. "I'm not sure I can tell him. It's too embarrassing."

"He'll help you if you'll work with him."

I sighed. "I never thought I'd have a problem like this."

"Nobody ever does."

I hadn't looked my dad in the eye since I'd admitted my problem, but now I did. We made eye contact. I could see his concern. It was reassuring to know he still loved me.

"All right, I'll meet with the bishop."

"Good. The battle's half won then."

"I hope that's true."

I thought we were done and my dad would take me home and then make arrangements for a later flight, and that within an hour he'd be gone for a couple of days. But the truth is, I didn't want him to go. I wanted him around. This was a problem that a dad and his son could work out. I wasn't sure I could talk to Lara about it. Or that, even if I did talk to her, she'd understand the temptation.

"Anything else that's troubling you?" my dad asked.

I answered too quickly. "No, nothing, everything's fine."

"Are you sure?"

"Nothing that I'd need to talk to my bishop about."

"Something else, then?"

"Nothing really important. We can talk about it after you get back from your trip."

My dad shook his head. "I'm not going anywhere today. This day is for you."

"So we'll work at the office with Mom, then, right?"

"No, let's take the day off."

"You never take the day off."

"Then I guess it's about time I did. How are you doing now? You want to just take it easy and rest, or do you want to do something?"

"I feel okay. I probably won't do any mountain biking for a while, but other than that, I feel okay."

"You sure?"

"Yeah, I'm fine."

"How would you like to go fishing?"

"We haven't done that for a long time. Sure, that'd be great."

Three hours later we were anchored in a boat at Strawberry Reservoir watching our lines, waiting for a fish to take our bait.

"These are the same fishing poles your . . . Charly and I used when we went fishing, before we were even married." He examined his reel. "You can tell this is old because it was made in the United States."

Twenty minutes later we hadn't even had a bite. "Having a good time?" he asked.

I did my best to be positive. "Oh, yeah, sure. Who wouldn't be having a good time. I mean, it's so quiet here."

He laughed. "You're a lot like your mom. She didn't like fishing either."

"Dad, can you tell me more about . . . my real mom?"

"What do you want to know?"

"Everything. Her parents let me look through some of their scrapbooks of when she was growing up. They told me lots of stories about her. I feel like I really need to know what she was like."

"Why?"

"Okay, look, I know it sounds like I don't love Lara, I mean, Mom, but that's not it. It's just that I'm not sure who I am. At work it's not as much fun designing Web sites as it was before my mission, and now I'm questioning if I even want to major in information systems. I mean, I keep thinking, what if I'm more like my real mom? I think the first thing I need to find out more about is what she was like and then, after I know that, maybe I'll be able to decide once and for all who I am and what I want to do with my life."

I didn't know how he'd react—if he'd be mad at me, or if he'd accuse me of not being grateful to Lara for all she'd done for me, or if he'd be upset that I didn't want to take over the family business.

"I'm going to put a new worm on my hook," he said, reeling in his line.

That made me feel as though what I had said was so bad that the only response he could muster was to pretend he hadn't heard me.

"You want to put a worm on your hook?" he asked me, handing me the can filled with soil and worms we'd bought from some kids in Heber City.

I shrugged my shoulders. "I can't see it'd do much good."

"Sometimes it does." He sounded optimistic.

While he cast again, I gave up and reeled in my line. A minute later, after putting a new worm on my hook, I cast out and let the hook sink to the bottom.

He studied his line, looking for any sign of a bite. I was surprised when he began to talk.

"When your mom realized she wasn't going to live much longer, the thing that was the worst for her was to realize you wouldn't remember her as you got older. You called me da-da, but you hadn't said her name. I remember one day . . ."

He paused. "It was near the end. I was in the kitchen peeling some potatoes, and I heard her. She was in the living room, and she was saying, 'Mommy, Adam, Mommy. Please say it. Please say my name.' But you crawled off and she broke down and she said, 'Adam, please say my name! I'm your mommy. Please remember me.'"

84

I wiped my eyes. I was glad we weren't facing each other.

He continued. "She loved you very much, Adam. And I'm sure she still does."

"Lately I've started to think of her as my *real* mom."

"You're lucky. You have two moms. And they both love you."

"I know. I love Lara too."

His eyebrows raised. "You're calling her Lara now?"

"Sometimes."

"She's your mom, Adam. She deserves a little respect."

"I know, and I do. I appreciate all she's done for me."

"I had a hard time after your mom died. I couldn't give you the love you needed. If it hadn't been for Lara, I don't know what would have happened to you and me. She's always been there for us."

"I know that . . . but I still need to know about my real mom. Dad, I'm not happy here. I want to go to New Jersey and stay with her parents and get my life on track again. They've invited me. I could work for Grandpa Eddie."

"What would you do?"

"He owns some apartments. He's asked me to help him with maintenance."

Dad reeled in his line and pulled up the anchor. I reeled in my line.

I couldn't tell what he was thinking, if he was mad at me, or if he thought I was being ungrateful for the love Lara had always lavished on me. Just before reaching the dock, he turned to me and said, "If you want to go for the summer, then go ahead. We can get someone who can take your place at work."

"Thanks for being so understanding."

He nodded. "We'll miss you."

"I know. Me too."

"Are you going to be able to stay away from pornography?"

"I think so. There's a lot I don't know about myself, but one thing I am sure of."

"What?"

"What I've been doing the past week is not who I am."

That night I called my grandfather in New Jersey and told him I would like to work with him until fall semester began.

"You mean it?" He moved the phone away from his mouth, and I heard him shout, "He says he'd like to come out here and work for me!"

I could hear Claire in the background. "Get out of here! Are you serious?"

"Talk to the boy if you don't believe me."

We talked for half an hour.

Dad and I told Lara what my new plans were. She seemed to take it personally. I felt bad about that.

Before going to bed, I packed up my computer and put it in the garage. Then I slept better than I had for several nights.

The next day I met with my home ward bishop. After we talked for a few minutes about my plans, he quit talking. I knew that was my cue.

My hands were sweating, and my stomach muscles were cramping. "I've had a few problems lately that I thought I'd better clear up before I leave town."

"What kind of problems?"

I lowered my head, trying to get enough courage to talk. "I never thought I'd have a problem like this."

I glanced at him, and he nodded his head but didn't say anything.

"Last week I stumbled on a porn site." I paused. "I knew it was wrong, and I tried to stay away, but I did go back—four times."

"How long has it been since you last watched pornography?"

I cleared my throat. "Monday night."

"I see. You obviously feel bad about this, Adam. What troubles you about what you've been doing?"

My face turned red. "It gives you bad thoughts, and, you know, it tempts you to do things you shouldn't do."

"And you want to escape this. Is that what you're saying?"

It was hard to admit such a thing, but I said, "That's why I came here. I want to quit and never do it again."

"Good for you, Adam."

He smiled at me. "I can see you're uncomfortable, but I want you to take a deep breath and relax. You took the biggest step when you admitted you have a problem. What we need to do now is work together to solve it. Are you up to that?"

I was afraid he was going to ask me to tell him about all the things I had seen, but I nodded my head.

"If you knew this was wrong after the first time, why did you go back?"

I had never felt more embarrassed than I did at that moment. "It was like I couldn't resist it."

"That's because pornography is addictive."

"I know that now."

"One of the strongest desires our Heavenly Father has given us is the drive to reproduce. If it weren't for that, the human race might have died out long ago. That yearning to have a mate is God-given and sacred and nothing shameful."

He continued. "What is sad is that the world sees sex only as something to be used recreationally and irresponsibly. With their pictures and movies, pornographers make something dirty out of something that is sacred and precious. Do you understand what I'm saying?"

I nodded.

"When a man becomes addicted to pornography, he has a difficult time relating, in a proper way, to women. He sees them as objects of lust, not as precious daughters of God."

I sighed. "I know." I told him about shooting baskets with Sierra and Kierra, and how inappropriate thoughts had

87

gotten in the way of the innocent fun we were having, so much so that I had to get away from them.

"Then you know what I'm talking about. And the truth is, if you don't control this, it will take over your life." He paused, and then repeated, "It will take over your life. It will also make finding a wife very difficult. And if you do marry and continue to feed your addiction, then there's a very real chance you can kiss your marriage good-bye. It might take a few years for your wife to find out, but when she does, she may even agree to work with you for a while, but, if you can't stop this activity, she'll lose respect for you and eventually seek a divorce. And when she leaves you, she'll take your kids, and you'll be left all alone with only a computer screen at night to keep you company. Is that what you want?"

"No, it isn't. I want a wife who will be able to trust me, and kids who will always be able to count on me."

"Then you know what you have to do."

"I do. And I will."

"Good for you. There's a scripture I'd like you to consider." He turned to Alma, chapter 22, verse 18, and had me read, " . . . if there is a God, and if thou art God, wilt thou make thyself known unto me, and I will give away all my sins to know thee, and that I may be raised from the dead, and be saved at the last day."

"Do you know who said this?" he asked.

"The father of King Lamoni," I said.

"That's right. How do you suppose this king was able to give away all his sins?"

"I don't know," I said. "I've never thought about it."

"Well, suppose he had dancing girls that performed at special dinners. What would he do?"

"Tell them he didn't need them anymore."

"That's right. That's how we overcome temptation. We remove the situations that lead to us being tempted."

"I'm moving to New Jersey to work for my grandfather. One

of the reasons I'm going is to get away from the computer. And I'm leaving mine at home. I've already boxed it up and stored it in the garage. So I won't be using the Internet at all anymore."

"What else will you need to do? What about watching TV late at night? What about renting inappropriate movies?"

"I'll stop watching TV and quit renting movies."

"Can you do that?"

I nodded. "I have to do it. I can't go back to any of this ever again."

"I'm happy you see what you have to do."

He assigned me to report to my new bishop and let him help me. And we had prayer together.

When I shook his hand and left his office, I felt much better. I felt like I could succeed, and that God would help me.

On my way home, I thought about "giving my sins away." The changes I needed to make were not just superficial, and not just for a week or two. I didn't trust me anymore. To make sure I stayed away from pornography, I knew I would have to sacrifice, and that would mean not renting videos, not watching TV alone late at night, and not using the Internet. I felt that I could do it; I just didn't know what I would do to fill the vacuum.

My dad and I went shopping for a used car. After a day of looking, we settled on a two-year-old Mercury Sable. He paid for it, and I agreed to pay him back.

At eight-thirty in the morning of Monday, June 3, I was packed and ready to go. My dad and Lara were hanging around the place to see me off.

Lara had gotten up early and baked me some blueberry muffins to take with me. She offered to cook me a big breakfast, but I told her I'd just have some cereal.

I made a few last-minute trips to the car and then went into the kitchen. Lara was cleaning up.

"Well, I guess I'm ready to go."

She was working at the sink and didn't turn around to look at me. "You'll call us tonight for sure, won't you?"

"I'm sorry for . . . feeling like I have to leave."

She turned toward me, and I could see tears in her eyes. "I understand why you want to learn about your first mom. As you work this out in your mind, Adam, please remember that I love you. I will always love you."

"I am sorry—"

"I know. It's okay."

The distance between us seemed like a million miles. I couldn't just give her a half-hearted wave and walk out.

"Is it okay if we hug?" I asked.

"Is it okay? Of course it's okay! It's what I want most of all."

We hugged for a long time and then it was time for me to go.

I went outside. My dad was trying to repack the trunk. When he saw me walking out to the driveway with my arm around Lara's shoulder, he gave up and slammed the trunk shut.

"It'll probably settle out during the trip," he said.

My dad and I faced each other.

"I got on a map Web site and printed you out the best route," he said. "It's on the front seat."

"Thanks."

We shook hands, then he pulled me into a hug.

"Be good," he whispered.

"I will, Dad. I promise."

"I know you will."

I got into the car, waved, and pulled out of the driveway on my way to New Jersey. True to my word, I left my computer at home. I felt as though I could do what the bishop had counseled me. Now the only thing left was to find out who I really was.

6

It was midnight when I pulled into the driveway of my grandparents' house in Madison, New Jersey. I was exhausted from having driven from Utah in three days.

The lights were on inside the house, but I didn't think my grandparents would be up this late. The night before, when we had talked on the phone, they had said they'd leave the door unlocked and the lights on, so I could get in no matter how late I arrived.

I grabbed a backpack and started for the door, deciding to unpack the rest of my stuff in the morning. I just wanted to get some sleep.

Inside the house, I'd only taken a few steps when my grandmother called from the living room, "Adam, is that you?" I looked in. She was sitting in a rocking chair with a quilt draped over her shoulders.

"You're up? You didn't need to stay up for me," I said. She stood up. We met in the middle of the room and gave each other a big hug.

"I was so excited I couldn't sleep. I'm so glad you made it here safely."

"Yeah, me too. It's great to be here."

"Let me show you to your room."

I followed her up the stairs. "We're so glad you're going to be with us for a while," she said. "Eddie has so many things he wants to do with you while you're here. Have you ever gone deep-sea fishing?"

"No, sounds interesting though."

"He wants to take you to a Metropolitan Opera concert in Central Park. I told him if you had any idea all the plans he has for you, you'd get right back in your car and drive home to Utah. Going here, doing that—but you know how he is."

We went upstairs and stopped at the first bedroom we came to. "We'd better tell him you're here. If we don't, he'll be after me all morning to go wake you up."

She opened the door. "Eddie, Adam's here. Do you want to say hello to him?"

The dark lump in the bed moved slightly. "What?"

"Adam's here."

He fought the covers to get out of bed. "Just a minute, I'm a little slow when I first wake up."

She laughed. "You're a little slow even after you wake up."

"I have my good days too." He stood up and cleared his throat and came toward me. "Adam, you're here! Did you have any trouble on the road?"

"No, everything went well." I braced myself as he threw his arms around me.

"I can't tell you how happy we are that you're here."

"Is it okay if I start work about noon tomorrow? I need to get some sleep."

"I wouldn't dream of having you start tomorrow. You need to rest up from your trip," he said.

"I'm okay. I could start tomorrow after lunch."

"We'll see. The important thing is you're here. How was the traffic?"

"Eddie, the poor boy needs some sleep. You can talk in the morning."

He said goodnight, and my grandmother and I continued on our way. We stopped at the bathroom, and she pointed out the towels I was to use. At the end of the hall, she turned on the light and welcomed me in.

"This was your mom's room when she was growing up. We got rid of most of her clothes years ago. I keep her scrapbooks here on the shelf and some of her artwork and a few other things in the closet that I just couldn't bear to throw away. And, of course, her harp."

The harp wasn't one of the huge kind but smaller, to fit a young girl.

"Your mother would not be pleased to know that of the few of her things we could have kept, we ending up keeping the harp."

She showed me the closet. It was empty except for some blankets on an upper shelf and some boxes and paintings in the corner. "Oh, your mom called last night. You forgot a few things. She's going to send you a package in a couple of days, so if you can think of anything else you need, let her know."

"Okay."

"How does she feel about you coming out here?"

"I think she's disappointed, but I think she understands I want to know as much as I can about my . . ." I sighed. "What do I call her? My real mom? And what do I call my mom now? My stepmother?"

My grandmother thought about it for a while. "Stepmother sounds like it's from *Cinderella*."

"Oh, yeah, the wicked stepmother, right?"

She nodded. "Both your moms have loved you, with all their hearts."

"I know."

93

"What if you called them your first mom and your second mom?"

"Okay. I can do that."

"What does your dad think about you coming out here?" she asked.

"I think he understands. He told me that my . . . first mom . . . when she was getting worse, he saw her trying to get me to say mama, and I wouldn't do it, and she started crying. My dad said the one thing my first mom feared was that I wouldn't remember her. And I didn't. But now, while I'm here, I'll find out everything I can about her. I think I owe her that."

"Do you think that maybe she knows about you being with us for a while?"

I nodded my head. "I've been thinking about that all the way out here. I hope she knows."

She looked at the clock. "Well, we'll have plenty of time to talk tomorrow. Right now you need to go to bed and get some sleep. Good night, Adam."

"Good night."

I slept until eleven in the morning. When I woke up, the house was quiet. I shaved, took a shower, dressed, and then went downstairs.

"About time you got up," my grandfather teased as I entered the kitchen. He threw his arm across my shoulders. "It's so good to see you."

They fussed over breakfast for me. They'd already eaten, but my grandmother cooked waffles and an omelet for me. It was more than I usually ate for breakfast, but they were so happy I was there and wanted to make my stay as nice as possible, I couldn't turn them down.

The next day I started working with my grandfather. He owned and managed three apartment buildings. My job was to help him do repair work. I liked the work and was glad to be learning skills that would come in handy when I had a home of my own.

On Saturday, after seeing the harp in my room morning and night, I decided to find out how to play it. I went to a music store and bought a basic book, and every night after work I practiced. When my grandparents realized what I was doing, they insisted I put the harp downstairs in the living room so they could listen while I played.

My brief problem with inappropriate Internet viewing went away now that I was staying with my grandparents. For one thing, I didn't have access to the Internet. My grandfather did have a computer with Internet access, but that was in his office in the garage, and I didn't go in there. My grandparents only watched home decorating shows or the History Channel. Occasionally I'd watch with them after dinner, but not more than a few minutes. And then I'd run for an hour, come home, take a shower, and then read the scriptures until I went to bed. That schedule made it easy for me to avoid any problems.

A few days later, just after getting home from work, I was practicing on the harp when I heard the doorbell ring. My grandmother answered it while I continued playing.

A minute later my grandmother and Brianna Doneau entered the room.

"Adam, you remember Sister Doneau, don't you?"

My jaw dropped and then I gave a lukewarm smile through gritted teeth. "Of course, how could I forget Sister Doneau?"

"You can call me Brianna now," she said, smiling.

"Yes, I suppose I could do that."

I hated to admit it, but she looked amazingly good. Her brown hair was cut in some kind of "young professional" look, and she was wearing a dark blue business suit that was probably very much in fashion. She seemed more relaxed than she had been as a missionary. Of course she'd never been relaxed around me on her mission, so maybe that wasn't an accurate assessment.

She wasn't wearing wire-rim glasses anymore. She'd finally joined the rest of the civilized world and gotten contacts. It gave me a better look at her eyes. I still found her combination of blue eyes and brown hair fascinating. Not that she could take any credit. I mean, let's face it, it was all in the genes. Still though, I found it hard not to stare at her.

"Adam, play one of your songs for Brianna."

I had only been trying to play the harp for a few days, teaching myself some simple melodies out of a beginner's book. The last thing I wanted to do was risk Doneau ridiculing me. "No, I'm done practicing."

"Please, just one song," my grandmother asked.

"Oh, I'd love to hear you play," Doneau said. I couldn't tell if she was serious or was mocking me. I was embarrassed to do it, but I played her one song.

"Wasn't that lovely?" my grandmother asked.

"Yes, it was, it was just lovely," Doneau said in a syrupy voice. Now it was clear, she was mocking me.

"Let me go get Eddie," my grandmother said. "He's in the backyard. I know he'll be thrilled to see you."

As soon as my grandmother was gone, I went on the attack. "What are you doing here, anyway?"

"I was in the neighborhood, so I thought I'd drop in."

"What do you mean, you were in the neighborhood? You don't live around here, do you?"

"Actually, I do. After my mission, your grandfather introduced me to a friend of his who has a law firm and was looking to expand. We hit it off well, and he offered me a position. It's a perfect situation for me with lots of opportunity. So I work and live in Newark, not far from here. Are you just visiting?"

Once again Doneau had everything going her way—a big-time job, and continuing access to my grandparents.

"No, I'll be here for the summer, working for my grandfather," I said.

"Well, we'll probably see each other then. Do you wish I hadn't come by to see your grandparents?"

I shrugged. "It's a free country."

"I love your grandparents and they love me, so that means I'll keep coming. I suggest you learn to deal with it."

"That's what I've learned to do when it comes to you," I said.

"If you want, in the future I'll call ahead and let you know I'm coming. That way you can go in the backyard and sulk until I leave. But for now, can you play me another of your lovely harp songs?"

"Let's get one thing straight, okay? I'm not a harp player."

"Gosh, you don't need to tell me that because I've heard you play. But, hey, if that's your thing, who am I to object?"

"For your information, the harp belonged to my mother. She took harp lessons when she was in junior high and then quit. It's been in her room since then. I'm learning to play it because I was hoping it would make me feel more connected to her."

Brianna sighed. "Sorry."

"Don't worry about it."

My grandparents came inside. My grandfather waved some tomatoes in our face. "We've got tomatoes!"

"I've called the *New York Times!*" my grandmother teased. "They should be here any minute."

"You have tomatoes from your garden? Isn't it too early for that?" Brianna asked.

"Not if you buy them in March with tomatoes already on the vine, and you put 'em in the window!" my grandfather said excitedly.

"And treat them like royalty," my grandmother said. "These are not just tomatoes. Oh, no! To Eddie, each one is like a member of the family."

"Stay for dinner, Brianna!" my grandfather said. "I'll put

tomatoes in the salad. It will be the highlight of your summer!"

Brianna already knew what my reaction would be to her staying. "Well, actually, I should be going."

"I wouldn't mind if you stayed," I said.

"You see that? Adam's heart will be broken if you don't stay!" my grandfather said.

"Please stay," my grandmother said. "If you don't, Eddie will spend the rest of the summer whining that you didn't get a chance to eat some of his precious tomatoes."

Brianna sighed. "Well, all right, if it's no problem."

Because my grandfather insisted on cooking the entire meal by himself outside on the grill, Doneau and I had a lot of time to fumble around at trying to carry on a conversation.

"So . . . how have you been?" she asked.

"Good, real good," I said. "And you?"

"Everything's fine."

"You told me once you had a guy waiting for you. How's that going?"

"Great. He's just finishing up his law degree. He'll be taking the bar exam this September."

"What's his name?"

"Thomas Marler."

"What do you like about him?"

"Oh, we have a lot in common. We both love music. And we have really stimulating political discussions."

I couldn't help being sarcastic. "*That* sounds exciting."

I thought that might get me a dirty look. Instead, Doneau looked kind of sad.

"So, does this guy come and visit you?" I asked.

"Well, he's been very busy."

"Yes, of course."

"He's doing job interviews right now. He's had several excellent offers already."

"So you don't see each other?"

98

"Not right now. We do e-mails though. Every day. Sometimes twice a day."

"That's good then."

"Now he just has to make up his mind where he wants to work . . ." She sighed. " . . . in Michigan."

"Michigan?"

"Yes, that's right. Probably Northern Michigan. That's where he's from."

"Doesn't it get cold in Michigan?"

"Just in the winter."

The conversation died again.

After a moment of silence, she asked, "Are you still mad at me?"

"I'm not sure now if I am or not. When I went home I was. I blamed you for ruining the last part of my mission."

"There's something you need to know. When I called President McNamara, I didn't ask for you to be transferred. I just told him what was happening."

"What was happening?"

She paused. "Nothing, I guess."

"That's right. Nothing was happening."

"You knew my first name, and one time you called me 'dear.'"

"I was being sarcastic."

"I guess I panicked. I'm so sorry if it made it hard for you. That was not my intent."

I nodded. "So, are you engaged now?"

"Not yet. As I said, he's preparing to take the bar exam. After he gets that out of the way, there'll be plenty of time for us."

"Well, that will be over soon enough, and then things will work out for you."

"I hope so, but sometimes I'm not so sure."

"Why do you say that?"

Doneau usually made eye contact while talking, but now

she looked away. "The thing is, he doesn't talk much about us getting married or having children. I thought he'd bring it up at least once in a while."

"Guys are like that. Don't worry. He'll be more relaxed once he's taken the bar exam."

She sighed. "Thanks. I appreciate that. I'll never understand guys."

"Anytime. Oh, by the way, you look good," I said.

"Thanks. You, too."

"I'm happier now than I've been for a long time," I said.

"I'm glad to hear that."

I laughed. "You know, being with you like this, it's hard for me to remember why I disliked you so much."

"It was because of my phone call you didn't get to see your grandparents' baptisms. I still feel bad about that, Adam." She cleared her throat. "Is it okay if I call you by your first name?"

"Yeah, sure."

"You do the same with me then, okay?"

"Brianna," I said, trying it out.

"Yes, that's right."

She stood up. "Well, maybe we'd better go outside and see if we can help," she said.

I followed her through the kitchen into the backyard. My grandfather was just putting the steaks on the grill.

"Is there anything we can do to help out?" Brianna asked.

"I've pretty much got things under control here," my grandfather said.

"If you want, you can make a salad," my grandmother said. "If you promise to be gentle when you slice the tomatoes. Eddie thinks of them as his children." She started laughing.

"We'll do our best," Brianna said as we headed back inside the house.

"Use whatever salad fixings you can find in the refrigerator," my grandmother called out after us.

"You're in charge," I said. "Just tell me what to do."

She broke into a silly grin. "If you only knew how much I used to hope you'd say that to me." She opened the refrigerator and began setting lettuce, radishes, green peppers, and baby carrots on the counter. "We really didn't get along very well, did we?"

"No, not at all, right from the beginning."

"Will you do the radishes and green peppers?" she asked.

We worked side by side for a few minutes without saying much.

"What do you do after work?" I asked.

"Why do you want to know? Are you asking me out?"

"No, not at all. My motto is never get between two hotshot lawyers who could bring legal action against you. I'm just curious, that's all."

"Well, I send an e-mail to Thomas every night. And then there's always work left over from the day. Let's see, what else do I do?" After a long pause, she said, "Oh, well, one thing, I'm taking singing lessons."

"Really? What kind of music do you like to sing?"

"Country western," she said with a straight face, and then started laughing. "No, just kidding. It's classical. I have a terrific teacher. She's worked with Metropolitan Opera singers, so she's very good. I'm lucky she agreed to take me on."

"So, are you a good singer?"

She shrugged her shoulders. "I don't know. Maybe . . . I'm good enough to sing in church anyway. I'm singing in my ward in a couple of weeks, if I can find an accompanist, that is. The music is very difficult. It's from Handel's *Messiah*."

The truth is that, because my second mom had insisted I take piano lessons when I was growing up, I realized I might be able to play for Brianna. I just wasn't sure I wanted to. Even though we were getting along well, I still had some resentment toward her.

All this time she had been washing the three kinds of lettuce we would be having in our salad, and having done that, she brought everything over to me. I thought it strange that in this big kitchen she would choose to work so close to me.

I think we were both aware of standing next to each other, although, of course, we didn't say anything.

When she leaned over to see how I was doing, she put one hand on my back. "You're doing a very good job."

"Thank you."

"I believe, based on your performance so far, that I might be able to trust you with the tomatoes."

"Oh, what a thrill! My life is complete now."

"Don't get your hopes up yet. I haven't come to any kind of final decision."

She leaned forward and turned her face toward mine, so we were looking directly at each other. "These are not just ordinary tomatoes, my boy."

"I know that. They are special."

"And they must be handled with great care and respect."

"I am up to the task."

"Well, all right, just don't drop them."

She walked ceremoniously to the counter where the tomatoes lay, picked up three, then pivoted, and tossed all three of them at me at once.

I managed to catch two, but dropped one on the floor.

She ran over to where the tomato lay on the floor, and got down on her knees to examine it. She tugged on my hand. "You get down here and look at what you've done."

We ended up on our hands and knees opposite each other, heads nearly touching as we looked at the tomato. It had split open on contact with the floor.

"How could you have been so careless?" she asked.

"You're blaming this on me?"

She made a silly expression. "Of course I am."

From the grill, we could hear my grandfather. "I forgot the Tabasco sauce."

"You don't need Tabasco sauce."

"Some people like Tabasco sauce on their steaks. I'll get some, just in case."

"He's coming!" Brianna cried out.

I grabbed the tomato from the floor and buried it in the pile of lettuce on the counter. Brianna started giggling.

"Shush," I demanded sternly before I also started to laugh.

By the time my grandfather opened the door and stepped inside, Brianna and I were busily working on the salad.

"How are you guys doing in here?" he asked.

"Good," I said quickly.

"Great. We'll be ready to eat in just a few minutes."

"Good," I said.

"Yes, good," Brianna said, and then started giggling.

"Do either of you want any Tabasco sauce with your steak?" my grandfather asked.

"Brianna does," I said quickly. "She likes things hot."

She looked at me like I was crazy.

"I'll get some then."

As he turned his back to us and opened a cupboard to look for the Tabasco sauce, Brianna moved the pile of lettuce to the side, leaving the damaged tomato visible for my grandfather to see if he were to turn around.

"Let's see, it's in here somewhere," he said, rummaging through the bottles on the shelf.

I pushed her away and covered up the tomato.

She slipped in, grabbed the tomato and dropped it on the floor. I picked it up and put it in a bowl.

My grandfather found the Tabasco sauce and then went back outside.

"What do you have to say for yourself?" I asked.

In her best Primary teacher voice, she said, "Adam, I really think you need to be honest and admit how you carelessly dropped the tomato on the floor."

"And you take no part of the blame in the tomato incident?"

"None whatsoever."

"I see."

I picked up the damaged tomato, rinsed it off under the tap, and began cutting so it could go in the salad. She, thinking the fun and games were over, went back to her work.

I cut up the two-thirds of the tomato that hadn't been damaged in falling to the floor. The remaining third I sliced into two parts.

"We need to destroy the evidence. Open your mouth."

She shook her head. "I don't think so."

I showed her the part she had to eat. "It's just this much. Open your mouth."

She opened her mouth, and I stuffed the entire piece in her mouth. She started giggling, grabbed the remaining damaged piece, and, after swallowing what was in her mouth, said to me, "Open your mouth."

I opened my mouth. She stuffed my share of the tomato into my mouth, then ceremoniously threw in some baby carrots and a radish. "You can close your mouth now and commence chewing."

I put one hand on the top of my head and the other on my jaw and pretended to try to shut my mouth. "I caan't doah dat."

She started laughing. "Don't talk with your mouth full."

We were both laughing, and then we turned to look at each other. Against our better judgment we kept looking long after we'd quit laughing.

"You look good too," she said. "Much better than I remember."

"I spend a lot of time outdoors, helping my grandfather."

"That must be it."

We ate at the patio table with the grill just a few feet away.

"If your steak isn't done enough, just let me know, and I'll put it back on the grill," said Grandfather.

"Mine's fine," my grandmother said. "I'm sure the others' are too. Sit down, Eddie."

"Is yours done enough, Brianna?" my grandfather asked.

"It's great. Just the way I like it."

"What about you, Adam?"

"Mine's good too."

"Because I can put it back on the grill if it's not exactly the way you want it," he added.

"It's great, really."

"Eddie, I swear, you're driving us all crazy!" my grandmother said. "Just sit down and eat."

"Oh, Brianna, here's the Tabasco sauce," my grandfather said.

"Yes, help yourself," I teased. "We all know how much you like it."

"You know what? This is such a good steak it doesn't need anything on it."

"Some people like steak sauce," my grandfather said, "but others don't. I've got A-1. I've got Heinz 57. I've also got Worcestershire sauce. Also, if you want, I've got ketchup."

"Eddie, I swear, this is the last time I'm letting you cook if you don't be quiet about the steaks," my grandmother said.

"My lips are sealed. You won't hear me say the word *steak* again this evening. Sister Doneau, how does your baked potato go with the dark brown broiled meat sitting next to it?"

Brianna burst out laughing. I very much liked that side of her.

At one point during the meal, we exchanged glances. She still had those amazing blue eyes. After a few seconds, we caught ourselves and turned away.

When we were nearly done eating, my grandmother said, "Guess what we're having for dessert."

"Cannoli?" Brianna asked.

"That's right. All you can eat."

"Wow. I'm so glad I dropped by."

"We're glad you did too. Aren't we, Adam?" my grand-mother asked.

"Yeah, actually, I am."

After we finished eating, Brianna and I helped clean up. I told her I was staying in the same room my mom had been in when she was growing up. "I've been going through some of her things. You want to see what I've found?"

"I'd love to."

I went up to my room with a couple of empty boxes from the garage and grabbed everything that belonged to my mom and then hauled it all downstairs to the kitchen. Brianna and I sat at the kitchen table and started going through it. I'd also brought some paintings my mom had done when she was my age.

"She was beautiful, wasn't she?" Brianna said, looking at a photo.

"Yeah, she was."

"What's it like for you to be staying in her room?" Brianna asked.

"It's hard to explain. Sometimes it's almost like she's here."

"And what's that like?"

"Very peaceful."

"She must be proud of the way you've turned out."

"I hope so."

Brianna pulled a *Monopoly* game from one of the boxes. "I haven't played this since I was a little kid."

"You want to play?"

"Sure, let's go see if we can talk your grandparents into playing too."

We played on the kitchen table. The four of us started out eager and hopeful, but, by ten-thirty, my grandfather was bankrupt and my grandmother was dozing. They excused themselves.

By midnight I was broke, trying to make it around one time so I could collect two hundred dollars. Unfortunately, I landed on one of Brianna's holdings–Boardwalk. "Uh . . . I'll need a loan," I said.

"No, what you need is a miracle. Let's call a truce, okay?"

"All you have to do is ask me to pay what I owe, and you win."

"I don't want to win this game."

"What do you want?" I asked.

"I'm hoping to get a friend out of this."

"Oh, and clobbering me at *Monopoly* is the way to do that?"

"Something like that. Can we quit now and maybe talk?"

"Sure."

We carefully put everything in the box, treating the pieces and cards with more respect than we normally would because they had belonged to my mom.

"Is it okay if I explain why I was such a control freak on my mission?" she asked.

"You were fine. Really."

"Still, I'd like you to know."

"All right."

"I grew up in Denver, Colorado. When I was a freshman in high school, my dad left my mom and me for another woman."

"I'm sorry."

She shook her head. "He took everything. He cleared out the checking and savings accounts, took our only car, and all the money we'd set aside for rent."

She lowered her gaze. "My mom was devastated. She had no skills, no education. She got one job working in fast food and a second job in a grocery store. We had to move to a cheaper apartment. We had nothing. It didn't seem fair that he could do that. My mom tried to collect child support, but the legal system seemed powerless to help us . . . because we had no money to pay for a lawyer."

"Is that when you decided to become a lawyer?"

She nodded her head. "I wanted to be an advocate for those who had no voice. It's what I still want. But first I need to pay off my student loans, and then I'll start my own practice and go after the bad guys."

For the next few minutes she told me how she had dedicated her life to getting good grades so she'd be eligible for scholarships, and how hard she'd worked to get through school as fast as she could.

She continued. "I had scholarships all the way through college." She sighed. "And then . . ."

"What?"

"Looking back, I can see I should have gone to law school in Colorado, but . . . I did so well on my exam to get me into law school, that I talked myself into going to the very best school that would accept me. And that was Columbia University. The scholarship pool, at least for me, dried up, so I had to take out school loans."

"You're doing okay, though, right?"

"Yeah, sure. I've got a good job here, so I'll just keep working until my loan is paid off. That might take two or three years, but I'll get it paid off and then I'll be free to do what I want to do."

"I still don't understand why you went on a mission after you finished law school."

She let out a big sigh. "Two weeks after I passed the bar exam, my mom was in a car accident. She never regained consciousness. She died two days later." Her eyes were glistening with tears.

"I'm so sorry."

She nodded. "Thanks. I'm okay now, but at the time I fell apart. I'd put all this effort into trying to make it right for my mom, and all the moms like her in the world . . . and just when I was in a position to begin doing it, she . . . died."

There was a set of crystal salt and pepper shakers on the table. She picked the salt shaker up, and grabbing a napkin from a wooden holder, slowly and methodically cleaned the finger marks from the glass.

"How did you get through all that?" I asked.

"Not very well. My dad and his second wife came to the funeral. I yelled at him at the cemetery and insulted his wife. I blamed him for everything bad that had ever happened to me and my mom." She sighed. "And then . . . I went back to our apartment and started to sort things out, what to keep, what to throw out, what to give to charity. Two days later the room was empty . . . and so was I."

She continued to fuss over the saltshaker. "My bishop and his wife came by a few days later. He asked me to consider serving a mission. He told me ward members would pay for it. I told him no at first, but then, after two months, I decided it might be the best thing for me."

"You never told anybody about this on your mission, did you?"

She shook her head. "I didn't want people to feel sorry for me."

I rested my hand on hers. "Thanks for telling me."

She nodded. "I just wanted you to understand why I came across as a little strange on my mission."

"How did Thomas come into your life?"

She sighed. "I almost hate to tell you."

"Why? You didn't meet him in a bar, did you?"

She smiled. "No, nothing that exotic. It was while I was at Columbia Law School. I had zero social life, but one night, in a weak moment I guess, I visited a Web site for LDS singles. In our biographical information, we both listed we wanted to be lawyers. So that's how we started e-mailing each other. He was a senior at Michigan State. I guess if my mom hadn't died,

109

we'd be married by now." She sighed. "Life doesn't always turn out the way you'd like."

"I know."

She looked at her watch. "I'd better go."

I walked her out to her car.

"Thanks for a fun night," she said.

"It was the tomatoes that did it for us, wasn't it?"

"Yes, magic tomatoes," she said with a slight smile. "Can you believe we're the same two people who fought so much on our missions?"

That made me laugh. "No. You're entirely different than I thought."

"You think we could be friends?" she asked.

"I'd like that very much. But there's something you should know about me."

"What?"

"I play the piano."

"No, you don't."

"I do. My second mom made me take lessons."

"You think you could accompany me at church on Sunday?"

"I could try. You want to get together tomorrow after work and practice? In fact, come for dinner."

"You will check with your grandparents about me coming, won't you?"

"I will, but they're crazy about you. I'm sure they'd love to have you."

"All right, tomorrow it is."

I opened the car door for her. "Good night, Brianna."

"Good night, Adam."

I watched her drive off, then went inside and hauled the harp upstairs. No more embarrassing, unscheduled concerts for me. Next I carried the two boxes of my mom's things to my room. In putting everything away, I was impressed with the paintings she had done.

Maybe I could do this too, I thought.

I grabbed a sketchpad and tried to draw a headshot of Brianna. It turned out awful, but it had enough promise that I felt if I practiced, I might be able to make a portrait of her good enough to give her as a present.

A few minutes later, after saying my prayers and crawling into bed, I started to think about my first mom.

It was a weird impulse, but I wanted to talk to her, so I pulled a quilt from the foot of my bed and I went to her closet and sat down.

It would have been too strange to talk to her out loud, so it was more like thinking than talking. But in my head I told her I wished she hadn't got sick and died. I told her I wished I could meet someone who was like her, someone who knew how to enjoy life and have fun, someone who would make me laugh, someone who would make me happy, someone like Brianna who I could talk with about anything.

I told her I felt sorry for Brianna, who had been first abandoned by her dad and then had lost her mom to an accident.

I told my mom I was beginning to think I was more like her than I was like either my dad or Lara. I told her I wished there was some way I could know if she'd heard me and if she understood.

I waited for an answer. But nothing happened. So I went back to bed and soon fell asleep.

In the middle of the night, I awoke to the sound of a harp being played. It was so real, that I sat up in bed. The room was dark, but for an instant it looked as though a woman dressed in a flowing white gown was seated at the harp, gently strumming it.

It seemed like the answer to my wish, that my first mom had come and was playing her harp for me. I wanted it to be her because I wanted to know that she still cared about me. And I wanted her to know that I was learning about her and that her hope that she would be important in my life was coming true.

I'm not sure how long I lay in my bed, trying to extend the fantasy, but eventually I noticed the wind was blowing, and every time there was an especially strong gust, the blinds and curtains would billow into the room, touching the strings of the harp and making a small sound.

It's just the wind, I thought. *That's all it is.*

I got up and shut the window and went back to bed and soon fell asleep for the rest of the night.

7

The next morning, my grandfather and I did some yard work at the apartments. Eddie had an old pickup truck with a trailer hooked on, which he used to haul his mower and other tools. He asked me to mow the lawns while he worked in the flower beds.

I was hot and sweaty after I finished, so I sat down near to where my grandfather was working and guzzled water and ate an apple.

He said, "Hard to beat a job like this, right? Here we are, as free as a bird. We're not stuck in some office. We're working on our tan, and we're enjoying Mother Nature."

A white-haired woman, well past retirement, walked briskly by us.

"Mrs. Emerson, how's your kitchen faucet working these days?" my grandfather cheerfully called out.

She seemed happy to see him. "It's worked just fine since you fixed it, Eddie. Thank you very much."

"Glad to help out. Give me a call if you have any problems."

"I will. Thanks."

A few minutes later a little girl about five years old approached us, carrying a paper plate of cookies. Her mom stood at the door to their apartment, watching her progress.

"I have some cookies for you, Mr. Riley," she said with a big smile.

She was so excited that just before reaching us she let the plate tip enough that three of the five cookies accidentally slid off the plate onto the ground.

She turned and looked helplessly at her mom. She looked as though she was about to burst into tears.

"Oh, boy, there's nothing I love more than cookies that have been on freshly cut grass!" Eddie said with a big smile, reaching to swoop them up.

The girl looked confused. "You do?" she asked with big eyes.

"Are you kidding? They're the best kind. Could I have the ones on the lawn? Adam here can have the others."

"Wait a minute! I want the cookies on the grass too!" I complained.

"Well, Teresa, I see we have a problem. I want the cookies on the grass, and my grandson, Adam, wants the cookies on the grass too. How can we solve this problem?"

She thought about it and then smiled and tipped the plate so all the cookies fell to the ground.

"Good thinking! Now we can all have cookies that have been on the grass!" my grandfather said. "And I very much hope that you can join us too!"

He looked over at her mother, who nodded. "I'll come back in ten minutes," she said.

"Let's have a tea party!" I said.

The little girl and I sat cross-legged on the grass while my grandfather sat on a low retaining wall next to us. We ate cookies and drank our tea, which was just water from our water jug.

"I had a little girl just like you once," my grandfather said. "We had tea parties too, she and I."

"What happened to her?"

He nodded. "Well, she grew up and became a wonderful wife and mom, just like your mom is now, and just like you'll be some day."

That wasn't the whole story, of course, but enough to satisfy Teresa.

A few minutes later Teresa's mom called for her.

"Can I stay longer?" Teresa pleaded.

"I'm sorry, but we need to go to the store now."

"But we're having a tea party."

"You can have a tea party the next time Mr. Riley comes."

Teresa shrugged, said good-bye, and ran to join her mom.

We finished up there, went home for lunch, then drove over to another apartment building.

"So how do you like working here with me?" Eddie asked as we were driving.

"Actually, this may be the best job I've ever had," I said. "It sure beats sitting around putting together Web sites."

"Yeah, it's fun. You know what? Life is for fun. I learned that from your mom." We pulled into a parking spot at the apartment building and got out of the cab of the truck.

"So, how did you and Brianna get along last night?" he asked.

"We had a good time."

He smiled. "Glad to hear it. She's a fine person. She'll make some lucky guy a great wife."

"True, but it won't be me. She's practically engaged."

"You never know. That could change."

When she got off work that afternoon, Brianna came to my grandparents' for dinner. After we finished eating, she and I went to the piano to see if I'd be able to accompany her when she sang in sacrament meeting.

She propped up the book in front of me. I'd never seen so

115

many notes in my life. It was way beyond what I could play. I thumbed through the pages. "Who wrote this stuff anyway?" I asked.

"Handel," she replied.

"My gosh, did he get paid by the note?"

She laughed. "Maybe so. Look, let's just try some hymns."

Out of kindness to me, she had us do a few easy hymns. Then, after gaining some confidence in me, she said, "Let's try my favorite hymn."

She turned to "Each Life That Touches Ours for Good," sat down next to me on the piano bench, momentarily rested her hand on my back and said, "Whenever you're ready."

I wasn't prepared for her singing voice. It was clear and pure and beautiful.

I made a mistake. "Sorry."

She leaned into me. "It's okay."

We started over. A short time later I messed up again. "Look, I'm not good enough for you. You need someone with, oh, I don't know, actual talent."

"You're doing okay. Really, and I'm sure you'll get better."

"I don't want to ruin it for you. Maybe you ought to ask someone else."

"Hey, don't worry about it. We'll practice until we can do it without any mistakes."

The next time we made it through the first verse with no problem.

The second verse went okay too.

I was excited as we began the third verse.

"'When such a friend from us departs, We hold forever in our hearts,'" she sang, and then she stopped.

"Did I do something wrong?"

She didn't answer. I turned to look at her. There were tears in her eyes.

"Sorry." She used her thumb to brush a tear from her cheek.

"You okay?"

"Yeah, I'm okay."

"You don't look okay."

"I'll be right back." She stood up and left the room but came back a moment later, carrying a box of tissues. She plucked a tissue then put the box on top of the piano and sat down next to me again.

I didn't know what to say and sat staring straight ahead, as if I were concentrating on the music. When she didn't say anything, I glanced over at her. She was gazing idly at the piano keys.

Finally, she took a deep breath and said, "This song always reminds me of my mom. I miss her so much. I could always talk to her about anything. She knew me better than anyone else. Even in high school, when girls usually distance themselves from their moms, I'd come home from school and tell her everything. She got me through some really hard times."

"How did it help to talk to her? Did she give you the answers you were looking for?"

"Not really. Mostly she just listened to me. That's what helped the most."

I could do that, I thought. *I could do that for Brianna. I could just listen.*

It was as if the thought had come from outside of me, encouraging me to try to listen to Brianna the way her mom would have done.

I wasn't exactly sure how to do it, but then I remembered the times when I would come home from school upset about something that had happened to me that day. Lara would listen and ask questions and then try to make me feel better.

Brianna began. "A few months after my dad left, we were living in a tiny apartment. My mom was working as a waitress, and we barely had enough money to pay the rent and buy food. Christmas was coming, and we had no money. A few days before Christmas, the bishop stopped by with two big boxes of food and presents for my mom and me."

"I bet you and your mom were happy to get some help."

"Yes, of course, but . . ."

"What?"

"In one of the boxes were some clothes for me. Some of the girls in the ward had donated them. The bishop hadn't told anybody who they were for, so the girls didn't know it was for me. And the things they'd donated were much more expensive than anything we would ever be able to afford. But once I realized where they'd come from, even though they were really nice, I went to my mom and told her I couldn't wear any of them."

"How come?"

"Because the girls would recognize them and know who was being helped."

"I didn't think about that."

"It was too much for me to take. I didn't want everyone to know how poor we were."

"I can see why you'd feel that way," I said. "So what happened?"

"My mom let me pour out my heart about how unfair everything was. I couldn't see how my dad could leave us and hook up with another woman and not miss a beat. The world seemed like it'd been set upside down. My dad had broken his marriage covenants, had run off with another woman, was living with her, and yet as far as we knew, he'd never missed a meal and always had the money he needed, while my mom and I were living on practically nothing. I remember saying, 'It's not fair.' And my mom said, 'Life is not always fair.' Maybe that's when I decided to go into law, to try to make life fair for other people."

"What happened to the clothes you were given?" I asked.

"That was an amazing thing. My mom altered them enough so the girls who gave them to me wouldn't even

118

recognize them. It took her hours to do. And she was already working long hours anyway, but she'd come home every night and sew. It must have taken her a week, but when she was done, everything looked so good. I had girls in church coming up to me and asking me where I'd bought the dress I was wearing. And, for all I know, that girl might have been the one who donated it."

"I wish I'd known your mom."

"Thanks. I wish I'd known your mom too."

We talked for thirty minutes before we started the third verse again. She asked me to sing with her.

"I don't think so. I'm really not a singer."

"Please."

I sighed. "All right."

We sang the fourth verse.

> For worthy friends whose lives proclaim
> Devotion to the Savior's name,
> Who bless our days with peace and love,
> We praise thy goodness, Lord above.

When we finished, she reached for my hand. "I think you are the kind of a friend who blesses your friends with peace and love."

"I'd like to be that kind of a friend to you."

"I can use all the friends I can get."

"Me too." I said.

She pulled her hand away. "Maybe we should do another hymn," she said.

I looked at my lonely right hand. "I could play one-handed if you want."

She playfully elbowed me in the side. We started through the hymnbook, finding here and there a song to do.

We sang for another half hour.

There was something besides music going on that I think

we both felt. Something neither one of us dared comment on. It had to do with being physically close to one another. It's hard to describe except to say that our bodies were somehow aware of each other. Not in an inappropriate way, and not something we would even mention to each other but, as we sat there, when we would lean against each other, or our arms would brush, or when our shoulders touched, or when she put her hand on my back to reassure me that I wasn't that bad of a singer, the simple touch seemed to be amplified a hundred times.

Some people call it chemistry, but whatever it's called, it's what we had going on between us. We didn't say anything about it, but there was no denying that it was there.

At nine o'clock she said she had to go. So we put away the hymnbook, and I walked her out to her car, where we stood and talked for another hour.

Just after ten, Brianna looked at her watch and said, "I've talked your ear off, haven't I?"

"No, not at all. I've enjoyed it."

"I've never known a guy who was so easy to talk to."

I smiled. The truth is I'd never been a guy people wanted to talk to. The amazing thing to me is that somehow, for the first time in my life, conversation had come easily. I was interested in what she had to say, and it was no problem knowing how to respond to her.

At eleven, she looked at her watch again. "Oh, my gosh! I'm really going now. Good night. It's been fun. I think we'll be ready for sacrament meeting on Sunday . . . if we can practice a few more times."

"Come for dinner tomorrow night."

"You're very free with dinner invitations when it's not your food and you're not the one doing the cooking."

I smiled. "How about if we help out?"

"Let's do the salad again," she said with a grin. "That was fun."

"Yeah, yeah." I pretended to shoo her away. "Look, are you ever going to leave?"

"See you tomorrow," she said, then got into her car and drove off.

♦   ♦   ♦

The next day, a Friday, Brianna called me on my cell phone while I was doing some routine maintenance at one of my grandfather's apartments.

"What are you doing?" she asked.

"Fixing a leaky toilet. What about you?"

"Oh, you know, the usual." She paused. "I was wondering if you'd like to meet me at five o'clock in Newark at my fitness club. We could work out together, if you're up for it."

"Yeah, sure. Just tell me how to get there."

Because I didn't want to be late, I actually got there fifteen minutes early and was immediately intimidated by the place. Everything, from the fancy exterior of the building to the green awning over the smoked glass front doors, spoke of money. Somehow my grandfather's pickup truck, with attached trailer full of yard tools and a riding mower, looked out of place in a parking lot filled with Jaguars, Lexuses, and BMWs.

When I reported to the reception desk in my faded jeans, baseball cap, and mission T-shirt, carrying a plastic garbage bag containing my workout clothes, the tall, blonde girl on duty gave me a skeptical look.

"I'm here to work out."

"Are you a member?"

"Uh, no. I'll be the guest of Brianna Doneau . . ."

The receptionist opened a black binder and asked, "How do you spell the last name?"

"D-o-n-e-a-u. Brianna."

She was so tall, I wondered if she was standing on some

kind of platform, and she looked down at me as though I were some sort of, I don't know, maintenance man.

" . . . but I guess she's not here yet," I offered.

She found the name and closed the book.

"I can't let you in until she vouches for you."

"Right."

She was wearing a black stretchy outfit and looked very fit. For some reason, I kind of started to babble.

"I just moved here. I'm from Utah, but my Grandpa Eddie wanted me to work for him, so I moved back here for the summer. I've never been here before. I mean, not right here in this gym. But I was on a mission here for my church . . ."

I could see she didn't want to hear any of it, and I glanced around the luxurious lobby. There were some easy chairs grouped around a low table with a huge vase of fresh flowers on it.

"Well, maybe I'll just, uh, sit over there and wait. If that's all right."

Maybe she felt sorry for me.

"I guess I could let you go in and get dressed, but if Brianna doesn't show up in the next few minutes, I'll have to ask you to leave."

She was wearing a nametag. "Thanks, Chanteuse."

"It's Chanteille," she corrected me.

I used an empty locker to change into my workout clothes, which consisted of a pair of worn, cut-off cargo pants and a plain white T-shirt, with my well-worn running shoes.

While I was getting dressed, I listened to the regulars as they changed and talked. They lived in a different world than mine. Most of them were my age or a little older, and they had obviously all worked hard sculpting their bodies. They looked good and they knew it.

Mostly they talked about their workout regimens. But one toned guy was complaining to his friend about how

122

incompetent somebody named Fletcher was. After a minute, I figured out Fletcher was their boss.

"There's no soap in the shower," a naked bronzed god told me as he walked by me. He obviously thought I worked for the fitness club.

"I'll get right on it, sir," I said.

That seemed to make him happy.

I went back out to the lobby to talk to Chanteille. "They're out of soap in the men's shower," I said.

"Why are you telling me that?"

"If you give me some soap, I'll take it in."

"We have people who do that."

"Great. So where are these people?"

She paged a guy named Roy Patterson several times with no success.

"Just give me the soap, and I'll put it in the guys' shower," I said.

She shrugged. "I don't really know where the soap is. We have a person who does that."

"Well, all I can say is that the guys are taking showers and there's no soap. How about if you go into the women's shower room and grab some soap, and I'll take it into the men's shower area."

"I don't think I could do that, sir."

I nodded my head. "You know what? You're probably right."

Just then Brianna came rushing through the door. My first impulse was to give her a hug, but I didn't do it for several reasons: First, some of the restraints from our missions were still on my mind. Second, she might not want Chanteille and the gang thinking we were more than friends. And third, of course, had to do with Thomas. I mean, Brianna had made it clear she was practically engaged.

But she seemed to have no reservations because she gave me a quick hug. "Sorry I'm late," she said.

"No problem. Chanteille and I have just been visiting. Right, Chanteille?"

Chanteille gave a forced smile that lasted a fraction of a second before she turned to answer the phone.

Ten minutes later Brianna led me to a row of glistening exercise machines. Most were occupied by sweating, robot-looking individuals with grim expressions, who did their designated reps and then silently moved to the next station. Each one had a water bottle and a towel. The machines faced a mirrored wall so the clones could each admire his or her body.

"So, how often do you come here?" I asked.

"Usually every day after work."

I nodded. "Okay, sure, well let's get started."

We started at one end of the machines and worked our way down the line. We finished on some treadmills. I hated to admit it, but Brianna was in much better shape than I was. It was hard work keeping up with her, and by the time we finished, I was sweating and breathing hard.

"Are you all right, Adam? You look like you're hurting."

"It's the way I always look, just before my heart attacks," I gasped, bending over and resting my hands on my knees.

I glanced up at Brianna. She was perspiring but otherwise looked relaxed. In fact, she had a very healthy glow about her.

"Do you want to sit down for a minute?" she asked.

I straightened up and forced a grin. "No. I'm okay. Are we through now?"

"I've had enough." She looked up at a clock on the wall. "What time are your grandparents expecting us?"

It was just after six-thirty. "I told them we'd be there about seven o'clock, but they said there's no special hurry."

We agreed to meet in the lobby, and then we separated to take showers and get dressed.

Brianna followed me in her car to my grandparents' place. As usual, they were happy to see her again, and both of them gave her a big hug.

Brianna and I insisted on preparing a salad. This time we didn't drop any tomatoes but just talked about our day, like we might have done if we were a married couple.

It was very comfortable for me—standing next to her at the sink, working together, tearing lettuce, and slicing vegetables and putting them in a bowl. She was apparently comfortable too because she would occasionally lean into me as she reached for something or rinsed her hands.

We didn't say a word about it though. To do so would have been to admit we were strongly attracted to each other. And that simply wasn't possible because she was practically engaged.

Maybe I wanted to punish myself. As we worked, I asked, "So, how's Thomas?"

"Good, real good. Oh, he likes to give me brainteasers with each e-mail. The one he sent this morning was so clever. What does a woman mining engineer say who finally gets rid of the guy she was going with whose first name is Tavias?"

"I have no idea."

"I got rid of Tavias on ore-bus!" I swear she actually laughed.

I shook my head. "I don't get it."

"Well you've heard of writ of habeas corpus, right? So it's like a takeoff. Writ of habeas corpus, which sounds like I got rid of Tavias on ore-bus. He made that up himself."

After a few seconds of bewildered silence, I burst out, "Really, well, imagine that." I forced myself to laugh.

"He sends something like that every day. Lawyer jokes too."

"Gosh, it must be a laugh a minute with him," I said.

"It's more cerebral humor than anything else. He's very smart."

125

"I can tell just by that one joke that he is."

We enjoyed eating dinner with my grandparents. They obviously cared a great deal about Brianna and seemed to be happy that she and I were getting along so well.

After dinner, Brianna and I ended up at the piano in the living room. First we practiced "Each Life That Touches Ours for Good." She had decided to sing it Sunday for sacrament meeting. We went through it several times, until we were able to do it with no mistakes. And then, with my grand-parents sitting nearby, we sang together some other Church hymns.

At ten my grandmother showed us a stack of music and invited us to go through it. "You might find something you'd like to sing." We had family prayer, and my grandparents excused themselves to get ready for bed.

Brianna and I had a snack in the kitchen and then wan-dered back to the piano. We went through the stack of music together. One of the songbooks had my mom's name written on it. It was the score of the musical *Carousel*. We also found a tattered script with Julie Jordan's part underlined.

"I think my mom played this role when she was in high school!" I said.

"Great, let's sing some of the songs."

I played as we sang four songs from the musical, but the one that meant the most to me begins "When you walk through a storm, hold your head up high. . . ."

After that, we just stayed at the piano, still facing the keys, I guess because Brianna could justify spending time with me late at night if we were involved in music. How could Thomas object if we were just singing together?

"You want to exercise with me again?" she asked. "I'll probably go tomorrow around noon."

"No thanks."

"Didn't you like it?"

"Not really."

"Why not?"

"I don't know. Everybody seemed so phony. Like working out is the most important thing in the world. And is it really necessary to watch yourself in a mirror as you go through each exercise? What's that all about?"

"It helps you see if you're doing it right."

"To me, it just seemed like all those people are in love with themselves. That's no way to live."

"Do you ever work out?"

"When I got back to Utah after my mission, I started mountain biking on some trails above our house. It was a good release for me. It helped me work through the frustration of creating Web sites all day."

"What do you do now to deal with your frustrations?" she asked.

I smiled. "I don't have any on-the-job frustrations now. This is the best job I've ever had."

She told me about some of the frustrations she was having at work—a boss who didn't give her credit for her efforts, always being given busywork that made a more senior member of the firm look good, having to work with people who didn't share her beliefs about the importance of being faithful in a marriage.

I tried to be a good listener, and I did my best not to offer any quick solutions to her problems. I just listened and tried to react to her the way her mom might have done if she'd been alive. It wasn't easy but I did it.

"You're so good for me, Adam," she said. "I feel better now. Thanks for listening."

"Yeah, sure, any time."

She looked at her watch. "It's late. I'd better go."

She stood up, but I reached out and grabbed her hand. "Let's go through this other book," I said.

"No, really. I need to get home. Thomas has probably sent me an e-mail."

The tone of her voice had suddenly changed, and I wondered if she was feeling guilty for spending the evening with me.

"I'll walk you to your car," I said. We were still holding hands and acting like it was no big deal, but it was. And we both knew it.

As we walked outside, I said, "I enjoyed singing with you tonight."

"Me too. It was . . ."

"It was what?" I asked. She didn't answer, but left me standing on the curb and walked around to the driver's side, unlocked the car door, and opened it.

"You want to do something tomorrow night? Go to a movie or something?" I asked.

"I don't know, Adam. Why don't I call you?"

I sighed. "Okay."

"But could we practice again, before my sacrament meeting?" she asked. "It begins at nine."

"I don't even know where you meet."

"How about if I pick you up at seven-thirty and then you won't have to worry about finding the place? And that'll give us time to practice in the chapel."

"Okay, great."

She looked at me across the top of the car. "Adam, I am totally committed to Thomas."

"I know. Sorry about . . . you know—"

"It was my fault. It's just that I feel very comfortable with you."

We said good night. She drove off. And I went to my room and drew another sketch of her. It was good enough to keep. I put it in my closet behind my mom's artwork.

In my bed with the lights off, I wondered how much my first mom knew about my life. I wondered if she knew about Brianna and, if she did, if she approved of her.

I wished I could talk to my first mom, but I didn't feel like

128

getting in the closet again to talk to a woman who had been dead for nearly my whole life. I decided that if I wanted to talk to anyone about my life, it should be Heavenly Father.

So I said my prayers and went to bed.

8

At two-thirty the next day, a Saturday, I was mowing the lawn at one of the apartment buildings when I got a call on my cell phone. "What are you doing?" Brianna asked.

"Mowing the lawn. Maybe lawyers can waste the day, but I'm a working man."

"Yeah, right," she scoffed. "Can I come join you?"

We ended up together on the riding lawn mower. I let her drive because I was too busy singing country songs at the top of my voice, including my favorite song, Willy Nelson's "You Were Always on My Mind."

"' . . . You were always on my mind, you were always on my mind . . .'" I wailed.

"You go, Cowboy!" Brianna shouted.

By the time I finished the song, she was laughing so hard she could barely keep the mower going in a straight line.

"You want me to drive?" I yelled over the sound of the mower.

"No, I'm okay. It's better now that you've stopped singing."

"What did you say? Is there something about my singing you don't like?"

"No, you sing okay. It's just I'm not a big fan of country."

"You stick with me, girl, and I'll change that."

"Thanks for the warning. So, let me ask you a question—is this what you call work?"

"Yes, of course. We're working very hard right now."

"It seems to me like we're playing."

"Life is for fun," I said. It was what my first mom used to say, and now it was becoming my motto in life.

After we finished mowing the lawn, we bought some fast food and came back to the apartment building and ate it in the shade of a tree.

My grandfather, when he worked around the place, was a kid magnet and because I worked with him, they treated me the same way. So before long we had six or seven kids around us.

We played "Clumsy Monster," a game I'd played with them before. Brianna and I were it, but, on purpose, we were so clumsy and slow we could never catch anyone. When one of them would get close, we'd lunge in slow motion to get them, and we'd miss time after time. The kids loved it, and squealed with delight.

Thirty minutes later, Brianna and I were both exhausted, and we told the kids we had to go. They begged us to stay.

"I'm sorry. But we'll come back real soon," I promised.

While Brianna kept the kids out of the way, I put down planks and drove the lawn mower into the trailer. As I was latching the tailgate, Brianna smiled at me and said, "You're way more fun than the people I work with."

"After what you've told me about them, that's not much of a compliment," I said.

That made her laugh.

It was a nice laugh.

She followed me in her car back to my grandparents'

house where I parked the truck and trailer. Then we drove to a park where we rented a boat. I rowed us out into the middle of the small lake where I began trying to row the boat in a tight little circle. I wasn't real good at it and ended up splashing a lot of water with the oars. Brianna sat in the back of the boat, facing me, trying to keep from getting wet, and laughing at my lack of skill. Finally, I gave it up and let the boat drift.

"What are we doing?" she asked.

"My mom and dad used to go fishing together before they were married. My grandparents told me all about it. My mom didn't enjoy it much, but she did it anyway."

"How come?"

"I don't know why. I guess maybe because my mom and dad were intrigued by each other."

"Intrigued?" she asked. "Is that the same thing as attracted?"

"Not in the beginning it wasn't."

"So what are we doing here, following in your mom and dad's footsteps?" she asked.

"That's right. Let's try an experiment. Let's be real quiet and see if anything happens."

"What do you think is going to happen?"

"I don't know. Some kind of magic I guess."

"I'll close my eyes." she said.

"Good idea. Me too."

After a minute, I opened my eyes. She was looking at me.

"So, what do you think?" I asked. "Anything magical happen?"

"I found out you squint your eyes like a little boy when he's told to close his eyes for a big surprise. It's kind of cute."

"A guy like me does not like to be called cute."

"Well, that's too bad. You are cute anyway, whether you like it or not."

"Do you want me to tell you what I like about your face?" I asked.

Suddenly she looked worried. "No, that's okay."

Then I knew what the problem was. She was afraid I might somehow let it slip that I cared about her. If I told her she meant more to me than the music we shared or the *Monopoly* games we played, then, because of Thomas, she'd be duty-bound to insist we quit seeing each other.

I liked her too much to risk that. I shrugged my shoulders. "Actually, I don't like your face that much. It's pretty much an average face in all respects."

She splashed some water at me and smiled. I think we were both relieved.

"The only thing I need right now is some shade," I said. "Let's take the boat back and do something else. This was a dumb idea."

"No magic, right?" she asked.

"That's right. Not a single bit of magic."

We spent the rest of the day with my grandparents, helping them do some yard work. And then, of course, they asked Brianna to stay for a barbecue.

After dinner, Brianna and I took a little walk. We ended up on the street that led to the train station, the one we had walked together several times while we were on our missions and going to or from my grandparents' house.

I thought about the battles we had had when we were competing over who was going to teach Eddie and Claire.

"Can you believe how we treated each other when we were missionaries?" I asked.

Brianna shook her head. "You were so rude," she said. "I could hardly stand to be around you."

I looked at her in disbelief. "Me? How about you? I had never met anyone more . . . more . . ."

"Spiritual?"

"No."

"Diligent?"

"No."

133

"Capable?"

I had been ready to take up the fight all over again, but when I looked at her, I could see she was just having fun, and it made me laugh.

"I know," she said. "I really *was* a pain. Always trying to protect my turf. I can't blame you for hating me."

It was my turn to apologize. "No. I was the one who was out of line. I was so insecure, I took everything personally. I'm sorry for the way I acted."

In the time since our missions, we had never really talked about the war we had fought. It was something we had needed to do. Now it had been put to rest.

She left at nine-thirty, promising to pick me up at seven-thirty the next morning for church.

Sunday morning, promptly at seven-thirty, I saw her pull into the driveway. I grabbed my scriptures and headed out the door to join her.

"You look nice," I said.

"You too."

"Are you nervous?" I asked.

"A little. How about you?"

"Yeah. You've got such a good voice. I don't want to mess it up for you."

"You won't."

"If I do, I'll stand up afterwards and take full responsibility."

She patted my arm. "Don't worry about it. Everything will go fine."

"Thanks for letting me do this with you."

"Are you kidding? It's been so much fun . . . to practice together."

"Yes, it has," I said.

"Oh, I got an e-mail from Thomas last night."

"How's he doing?"

"Really well. He asked about you."

"What did he want to know?"

"Oh, you know, just the usual. Like why I'm never home when he calls."

"What did you tell him?"

"I told him about us practicing for today."

"Sure, we had to practice a lot because I haven't played since high school."

"I told him that."

"Good."

"I think he was a little jealous," she said.

"Of me? No need for that."

"That's what I told him."

"Good. I'm glad you did. I wouldn't want Thomas worrying about us. I want all of his energy focused on passing the bar exam."

"I agree . . . totally."

We were early enough that we had the chapel to ourselves. First Brianna warmed up. Then we went through the song a couple of times, and then had a short prayer.

We decided to sit in one of the side rows near the front. The meeting wouldn't start for another half hour, so we each opened our scriptures and spent time reading. As the people began coming in, I wondered if someone walking into the chapel and seeing us sitting next to each other would think we were a couple. I could see how that could happen because of how close we were sitting to each other.

Our part of the program turned out much better than I'd even hoped for. I managed to make it through with only one tiny mistake. Brianna's amazing voice filled the chapel with beauty, and, even more important, it brought the Spirit into the meeting.

When we sat down again after we finished, she reached for my hand and squeezed it and leaned over and said quietly, "Thanks. You did great."

"No. *You* did great!" I whispered.

She nodded, and I put my arm around her and gave her a squeeze. For an instant she relaxed in my arm, but then she moved a few inches away.

During Sunday School, we sat in the first row and both participated in the lesson by answering questions and giving comments.

It was a substitute teacher, and he didn't know who we were. "Let's see, you're Brother and Sister . . . ?"

"Actually, we're not married," I said.

"Oh, sorry."

"No problem," Brianna said. "We both enjoy music. That's what brought us together."

I nodded, seemingly in total agreement.

After church, on our way out of the parking lot, Brianna turned to me and said, "Since we're over here, would you like to see where I work?"

"Yeah, sure."

Twenty minutes later we got out of the elevator on one of the upper floors of an office building. She unlocked a door and led me into a suite of offices. Her office was actually a cubicle surrounded by other cubicles.

"This is home," she said.

I couldn't help noticing her desk was clean.

We moved a chair from the adjoining cubicle so we could both sit down.

"So, what do you do here all day?"

"Mostly I do research for one of the more established lawyers. As soon as I get a little more experience, they'll give me more responsibility. But, actually, this is only a temporary job. When Thomas and I get married, we'll be living in Michigan. His dream for us is to some day have our own practice." She paused. "Some day he hopes to run for governor."

"It's great you both know what you want to do. I was going to major in information systems, but now I'm not so sure."

"What would you rather major in?" she asked.

"Well, that's just it. I'm not sure. It's been so much fun working for my grandfather. If I could, I'd just keep doing this for the rest of my life."

"You're so smart though. You could do anything you put your mind to."

"What's the point of doing something your whole life you don't enjoy?" I asked. "Do you love everything about your job?"

She looked around her tiny cubicle. "Some things you do because it's like you have to pay dues to get where you want to go. That's what this job is for me. It's just a stepping-stone to something I really want."

"And what is that? To make a lot of money?"

"No, to make a difference, to improve conditions for people, to be a champion for the underdog."

"How many underdogs come in here in a day? I mean, let's face it. The only people who can afford to come here already have lots of money. So what good are you really doing anybody?"

Her voice turned stern and unyielding. "I'll get to where I want to be, Adam. Don't you tell me I won't."

I'd said too much. "I'm sorry."

She stood up. "It's okay. Let's just go."

As we got in the car, I said, "So, how far do you live from here?"

"About ten minutes away."

"Could I see your place?"

She sighed. "I don't think it would be appropriate for us to be alone in my apartment."

"I just want to see it, that's all. I mean, it's not a big deal."

"I know." She sighed again. "But what if Thomas called while you were there? What would I tell him?"

"The truth. That we're just friends."

"I don't want him to be distracted while he's getting ready for the bar exam."

"Okay, no problem."

When we pulled into my grandparents' driveway, my grandfather came out to talk to Brianna. "How did you two do on your song in sacrament meeting?"

"We did great," Brianna said with a big grin on her face.

"I wish we could have been there, but they have us teaching Primary in our ward, and the kids would miss us."

"That's okay."

"You'll eat with us, won't you?"

She paused. "Well, the truth is I feel guilty eating all your food."

"Nonsense, we'd just throw it out if you didn't eat with us. Please stay. It'll be ready in just a few minutes."

I knew that Brianna was trying to put some distance between her and me, but it's very hard to turn down my grandfather, so in the end she agreed to stay.

We warmed up to each other a little bit while we helped my grandmother set the table and lay out the food.

We ate in the dining room. The food was good, and my grandparents took so much delight in having Brianna there, that she couldn't help feeling welcomed and loved.

Just after dessert, the phone rang. It was Lara, my second mom, calling from Salt Lake.

Because she had insisted on me taking piano lessons, one of the first things I told her was about the song we'd done for sacrament meeting.

She was delighted.

"You want to hear it?" I asked.

"I would love to hear it," she said enthusiastically.

We set the phone near the piano and did our song.

"Oh, that was so wonderful! Brianna has a beautiful singing voice."

"Here, I'll let you tell her that."

I gave Brianna the phone. "My mom wants to talk to you."

"Oh, yes, Adam is taking good care of me. He's such a nice guy. You must be very proud of him," Brianna said. They talked for ten minutes, and it made me glad they got along so well.

Finally Brianna handed the phone back to me.

"We got some mail for you from BYU," Lara told me. "Do you want me to forward it to you?"

"No, just go ahead and open it and tell me what it says."

"Hold on." A long pause. "It's an invitation to freshman orientation. You're supposed to RSVP. What shall I tell them?"

"I'm not sure."

"They'll need to know in two weeks."

"Okay, I'll think about it."

"Also, your father and I need to know if you want to work part-time for us while you're at BYU. You could do it from a computer at school."

I hated feeling that pressure from her. I hesitated for a bit, then said, "I'm not sure. I'll have to let you know."

Lara apparently thought I was worried about something else because she said, "We checked. They have filters that block pornography, so we think you'd be okay."

I felt embarrassed because it was the first time I realized my dad had told my mom about the problem I'd had before leaving home. Also, I worried that Brianna might be wondering why my face was turning red.

"Actually, on that topic, Mom, I'm doing really well."

"I'm so glad to hear that. We're proud of you for honoring your temple covenants."

"Mom, I need to go now."

"Think about working for us, will you? It'd be good for us and bring in some extra money for you."

"Okay, I will. Thanks, Mom. Nice talking to you."

When I hung up, I wondered if Brianna could tell I had felt embarrassed at what my mom had asked me.

She didn't seem to notice, probably because she had her own issues to deal with, namely that we were fast becoming very good friends even though she was planning on marrying Thomas.

"I'd better go," she said.

"Okay. I'll see you around. Is it okay if I don't walk you out to your car?"

"Of course it is. We'd just end up wasting another hour or two if you did."

"That's probably true."

I gave her a halfhearted wave after she'd thanked my grandparents and was on her way out the door.

I was in no mood to attempt another drawing of her. For one reason, I could never do her justice, and for another reason, I knew it was a waste of time to invest any feelings in a girl who was about to get married.

While my grandparents took a nap, I sat at the piano and played hymns and then, tiring of that, started to come up with a song. At first it was just a song reflecting how I felt, but after an hour I realized I was writing a song for Brianna.

It made me mad that I couldn't get her out of my mind, that whenever I had a moment to spare I'd start drawing her face or writing her a song.

I'm setting myself up for a huge disappointment, I thought.

9

On Monday, Brianna was too busy at work to come for dinner, but she did drop by a little after eight- thirty. We went into the kitchen and had cookies and milk.

"There's something I need to talk to you about," she said.

"Sure."

"Thomas called me last night after I got back to my apartment. He wants to come down and see me Friday night. If he comes, he'd stay Friday night and then head back sometime Saturday afternoon."

"I bet you're excited to see him," I said, trying my best to hide any jealousy I was feeling.

"Yes, I am. It's been a while since we've been together." She paused. "There's just one problem."

"What's that?"

"Well, of course he could stay in a motel . . ."

Suddenly I got it. "There's no reason for that. Why don't we see if he can stay here? I'm sure my grandparents would be happy to put him up for the night."

She nodded. "I've already talked to them about it. When

141

your grandmother called me at work to invite me to dinner, I told her Thomas was coming, and she insisted he stay with them." She paused. "The thing is, I wasn't sure how you'd feel about it."

"Look, you and I are just friends, okay? I'll be fine with him staying here."

"You're sure?"

"Absolutely. He can stay in the guest room. It's such a big house, we'll probably never even bump into each other and even if we do, we'll get along great. I mean, we have a lot in common. We both think you're wonderful."

And so it was arranged.

Although I'd said Thomas and I would get along, the truth was I didn't even want to meet him. I wouldn't have, either, if he'd kept to the schedule he and Brianna had arranged for his visit.

The plan was that Brianna would pick him up at the Newark airport at seven. She'd drive him to the house so he could meet my grandparents and drop off his stuff, and then they'd go out to eat. By the time they got back, I'd probably be in bed. They'd be gone most of the day Saturday, and then she'd drive him to the airport to catch a night flight to Detroit.

Early Friday evening, about the time his plane was scheduled to arrive, I was in the basement of one of my grandfather's apartment buildings, trying to bring order to the tenant storage room. It was a slow process that involved asking the tenants to come, one at a time, to the storeroom and identify their stuff, which I then tagged.

At nine o'clock, I figured Thomas had long ago showed up at the house and left with Brianna, so I drove home.

I drove past the house slowly to make sure Brianna's car wasn't there, went around the block, and then pulled into the driveway.

I had just gotten out of my car when Brianna pulled into the driveway.

I was trapped. There was no way out of it—I would have to meet Thomas.

He wasn't at all how I'd pictured him. Because Brianna described him as extremely bright, I thought he'd be like the bookkeeper who worked for Scrooge in Dickens's *Christmas Carol*—wire-rim glasses like she used to wear, somebody with no social skills. The kind of person who's stumped for a response if you ask, "How's it going?"

He was better looking than I would have preferred, and more at ease with people. He shook my hand and told me how much he had looked forward to meeting me, adding, with an almost snobbish smile, "Brianna's told me a lot about you."

"She's done the same about you."

"Where do you work?" Thomas asked.

"I work for my grandfather," I said.

"What firm?" he asked. He had an annoying tendency of standing too close while he talked.

"It's not a law firm. Actually, it's a *lawn* firm."

Brianna winced.

"What?" Thomas asked.

"I help my grandfather maintain some apartment buildings. You know, routine stuff: leaky faucets, leaky toilets, leaky roofs. Oh, also, I mow lawns. We've got a big riding mower. If you have time while you're here, drop by and I'll let you try it out. It's a beauty."

Thomas looked confused. He looked at Brianna as if he couldn't understand why she'd spend time with a common laborer. "Fascinating," he said.

He had little or no interest in me after that. He turned to Brianna again. "Let's get going."

While Brianna took him inside to meet my grandparents, I went around to the back of the house to wait until they were gone. There had been a big wind the night before, and there were some branches and leaves lying on the ground. I got a rake and some pruning shears from the garage and was cleaning them up when Brianna came out to talk to me.

I could tell she was mad by the scowl on her face. "What was *that* all about?"

"What was *what* all about?"

She imitated me. "'Oh, it's not a law firm, it's a *lawn* firm. If you want to ride my riding lawn mower, just come by.' So what part are you playing today, Adam, the lowly hired man?"

"That's right. That's what I am."

"Not to me, you aren't."

"Really? I find it interesting you never told Thomas what I do. Why's that? Ashamed to admit you're spending time with a guy who mows lawns for a living?"

"I can't talk to you when you're like this."

"You don't need to talk to me now, Brianna. Thomas is here. Why don't you go inside and hang on his every word?"

She shook her head and then went back inside, and a short time later the two of them left.

I figured they wouldn't be back until after midnight, so at eleven-fifteen I decided to get ready for bed so I wouldn't have to talk to Thomas.

I was brushing my teeth in the bathroom when there was a knock on the bathroom door. I opened it and Thomas came in.

His hair was all mussed up. "Whoa! What a night!" he grinned.

"Oh?"

"Oh, yeah. She was all over me. I'm serious! She just couldn't get enough of me. I did manage to hold her off, but it was all I could do to get out of her apartment."

I felt sick to my stomach. "Oh," was all I could say. I put my toothbrush in the cabinet and quickly left.

I couldn't sleep. I'm not sure what angered me the most: that Brianna would be, as Thomas said, "all over him," or that he would betray his relationship with her by telling me. Some things are best left unsaid.

On Saturday I woke up early, so I'd get away before Thomas got up. I didn't want more details of what had gone on with him and Brianna the night before.

I drove south, along the coast, playing tourist and scoping out the beaches, looking for places where I might come the next time a sunny Saturday came my way.

I found a great little place called Spring Lake, a picturesque beach town on the Jersey coast. Entering the small town was like going back in time. Large, white, three- or four-story houses, built generations ago, when times were good, lined the narrow streets.

In the middle of the town there was pretty little park with a pond and a picturesque foot bridge. It was a storybook village of vacation homes, tiny shops, and cafés.

I walked along the beach for an hour and then sat for a while on a bench in the park, watching people walking their dogs, playing Frisbee, riding bikes, and enjoying the sunshine. The pace of things was so unhurried and relaxing that I promised myself to return someday.

I tried not to think about Brianna and Thomas, but I couldn't get them out of my mind. I bought lunch from a hotdog stand near the beach and spent some time poking around in the souvenir shops. The whole time, I kept picturing Brianna and Thomas, laughing together, eating lunch, holding hands, and even kissing. It was driving me nuts, and I was relieved when I got home that night to find that Thomas had left.

On Sunday I went to church with my grandparents and then went home and took a nap.

Brianna phoned me around three in the afternoon. She told me she'd been asked to sing for a stake council meeting early Sunday morning on July 7, two weeks away. "I'd like you

145

to play for me. I was wondering if we could get together this evening and practice."

I was still mad at her. "Actually, I'll be busy the rest of the day."

A long pause. "The whole time?"

"Yeah, pretty much."

"Oh."

A prolonged silence.

"Maybe sometime during the week then, okay?"

"I might be busy then, too. Why don't you get someone else to accompany you?"

For the next few days I managed to avoid her. I didn't return her phone calls and stayed busy.

At ten-thirty on Friday night, she phoned me. "I hate to bother you, but I've got water leaking in my bathroom," she said. "Could you come over and look at it?"

I couldn't turn her down for that.

When I arrived, she was waiting for me at the door. She led me to the bathroom and stood next to me as I looked in the cabinet under the sink.

"Nothing's leaking now," I said.

"It was."

I stood up. We looked into each other's eyes.

"Can you wait until it starts again?" she asked.

"That might be a long time."

"I know."

"What's going on?" I asked.

"I've missed you."

I shook my head. "I find that hard to believe." I started for her door.

"Why do you find it hard to believe?" she asked.

I turned to look at her. "Look, let's not play games. Thomas told me what it was like being with you."

"What are you talking about?"

"Oh, get off it, Brianna. I really don't care what you two did together, but at least be honest with me."

"What did he say?" she asked.

"You are such a hypocrite."

"Just tell me what he said."

"He said you, and I quote, 'were all over him.'"

She looked shocked. "I can't believe Thomas said that."

"Why? Does it surprise you that he'd tell me?"

"No, it surprises me because it's a downright lie. We kissed once at the door, but that's all."

"So why would he make up something like that?"

She handed me her cell phone. "Let's call and find out."

I handed the phone back to her. "You call him, tell him what I said, and then let me speak to him."

She made the call. "Thomas, this is Brianna. I'm here talking with Adam. Did you tell him I was 'all over you'?"

A long pause.

"Yes, he's in my apartment . . . Yes, I know it's late . . . Well, I'm sorry you're upset that he's still here . . . Thomas, I'm upset you would say something like that to anyone about us. Did you or did you not say that to him?"

A long pause while she listened to him. She began tapping the tabletop with her fingernails.

"I don't know, Thomas. What do you think would be a definition of 'all over me.'? Well, I suppose it is a possibility that it merely meant I was happy to be with you, but usually, I think it has a far different meaning."

They wrangled like this for another five minutes, and then I grabbed the phone from her.

"Thomas, this is Adam. What were you thinking, telling me lies about Brianna?"

A long pause while he discussed things with his lawyer, which was himself. Then deciding that honesty might be the best policy, he said, "It was just a strategy to keep you two from seeing each other again."

147

"So you told me a lie about Brianna and you, just as a strategic move?"

"I wouldn't neccessarily categorize it as a lie."

"Thomas, with all due respect, you're a total jerk." I ended the call.

I turned to Brianna. "How can you have anything to do with someone like that?"

The phone rang. Brianna picked it up and said hello, and then said to me, "It's Thomas. He wants to apologize."

"To me or to you?"

"To me," she said.

"Sure, see you around."

The next day, Brianna called. She told me Thomas had apologized for what he'd said, and that she was sure he wouldn't ever do anything like that again.

"So you're back together?" I asked.

"We are."

"That's just great," I said sarcastically.

"Is there a chance you can accompany me when I sing next week?"

"I thought you were going to get someone else."

"I haven't been able to find anyone. Please, Adam, help me out."

I didn't want to do it, but in the end, I agreed to practice with her after church on Sunday. Of course, once my grandmother found out, she invited Brianna to have dinner with us.

On Sunday Brianna showed up at two-thirty in the afternoon. My grandparents said they were going to take an hour nap, and asked if we could do a few things in the kitchen.

I began peeling potatoes while Brianna was putting together a salad. For a few minutes, we worked in silence, then I asked, "So, how are things between you and Thomas?"

"We had a long talk last night, so things are good."

"You're still planning on getting married?"

"Yes, we are. Thomas explained what he meant by what

148

he said to you. He just meant we were happy to see each other again."

"Oh, sure, I see. It totally depends on your definition of 'She was all over me.'"

"He won't do it again."

"I still think he's a jerk."

We fell silent again. But after a minute or two, Brianna said, "Adam, can we still see each other?"

"What would be the point?"

"There is no *point.* I just enjoy hanging out with you. You're one of the best friends I've ever had."

It didn't seem entirely right, but I had missed her. So even though there was no future in it for me, I nodded. "It's okay with me if we see each other . . . until I go."

"Good. Thanks."

A few minutes later we started talking about sports, and I mentioned I was a big fan of the Utah Jazz. She started trashing them, so I quietly went to the sink and filled a glass with water, moved behind her, stuck my fingers in the water, and flicked some of it at her.

She turned to look at me. "Excuse me. But did you just throw water on me?"

"That's right. You got a problem with that?" I did it again, this time in her face.

She got a determined look on her face and said, "All right, no more Sister Nice Guy!" She turned to the sink, filled a glass with water, and began stalking me around the kitchen.

I backed away. "Brianna. You need to think this through. I'm sure my grandmother wouldn't appreciate you getting water all over the house."

She looked chastened for a moment and lowered the glass. "You're right," she said, "but she probably wouldn't mind my getting it all over *you!*"

With that she sprang at me and drenched the front of my shirt.

"Oh, is that the way it's going to be! You are in so much trouble right now!"

I stepped into the laundry area and got a bucket, then took it to the sink and began filling it with water. I turned toward Brianna.

Her eyes got big, and she backed away from me, holding her hands up in front of her. "No, Adam, this is a Sunday! What do we do on a Sunday?"

"We have a water fight!"

And that is what we did.

It ended outside with me chasing her around the yard with what she assumed was a full pail of water. Our hair and clothes were wet, and we were both breathing hard when I finally cornered her. She flinched as I drew the bucket back, then screamed and turned away as I tossed the imaginary water at her. As soon as she realized I had fooled her, she darted for the hose, but I stepped in front of her and held out my hand.

"Truce?" I asked.

She hesitated a moment, trying to decide if I was being sincere, then took my hand and shook it.

"Truce."

Laughing, we plopped down on some lawn chairs.

"That was so much fun," she said. "It's the kind of thing I hope my husband and I can do when we're married."

I found it interesting she didn't mention Thomas. Instead it was "my husband." I took it as a hopeful sign.

"It's the kind of thing my real mom would have done," I said.

"Probably so."

"I like it when I'm more like her," I said.

"I like it when you are too."

On Monday, Brianna invited my grandparents and me to her apartment for dinner and family home evening. Eddie and

150

Claire, of course, loved everything Brianna had done to decorate the place, and they raved about her cooking.

During dinner, my grandfather asked Brianna and me if we would like to go deep-sea fishing with him on Thursday, the Fourth of July. Brianna was enthused, and immediately said she would love to. I also said I'd go, but I really didn't want to. It was hard for me, being with Brianna, when I knew there was no future in it for me. It was great doing things with her, but Thomas's shadow was always there, reminding me she was already committed—to a guy I couldn't stand.

On Tuesday, Brianna phoned and asked if we could practice the song she would be singing for stake council on Sunday. I told her I could practice with her the next night at nine-thirty. I didn't tell my grandparents, though, because I didn't want them to invite her to eat with us. I just wanted to practice and be done with it.

The next night, it took only twenty minutes to rehearse the song.

"Well, you probably need to go," I said.

"Can we talk?"

"What do we have to talk about?"

"I need to ask your advice . . . about Thomas. Sometimes I don't understand him."

"And you think I do?"

"Please, Adam, as a friend, won't you help me?"

Just as I was trying to decide how to tell her I didn't want to talk to her, a thought came into my mind. *Help her out if you can. She doesn't have any family to go to.*

I sighed. "Of course I will."

We sat across the kitchen table with cookies and milk nearby.

"Sometimes I find it hard to talk to Thomas."

"How come?"

She thought about it. "I'm not sure. With him no conversation lasts more than thirty seconds. I tell him my concern,

151

and he gives me an answer. In his mind he's ready to move on to another problem, but I feel like he still doesn't know how I feel."

"That must be really frustrating," I said, not vocalizing any of the quick solutions that came to my mind.

"It is. I don't need him to solve all my problems. I just need him to listen to me." She paused. "Like you do."

"I'm glad I'm doing something right."

"He and I have so many things we need to talk about. We need to talk about when we'd like to start a family, but when I bring up the subject, it's like he doesn't have time to discuss it."

"Is he planning on giving birth to your children too?" I asked.

She smiled. "I'll ask him that the next time we talk." She put her hand on my arm. "You're the nicest guy I've ever known and the best friend I've ever had."

"Thanks."

"Another thing bothers me about Thomas. He doesn't like me talking about my mom. He says she's dead and that I need to get over it. He says it doesn't do any good talking about something that can't be changed. Maybe he's right, but I still feel a need to talk about how much I miss her."

She continued to talk about her frustrations with Thomas. I didn't have much advice for her, but she told me it had helped her just to be able to talk about it.

On Thursday, my grandfather took Brianna and me deep-sea fishing. We left early in the morning, and he paid for us to go on a charter boat. Brianna was the only woman. She caught two fish and was a big favorite with all the other men who were onboard. I didn't catch anything, but I did manage to get seasick in front of everyone. So it was a day I won't soon forget.

By Saturday, I was finally over feeling like I was pitching up and down on the deck of a boat, and just after noon,

Brianna and I drove to Spring Lake, the beach town I'd discovered the day Brianna was out with Thomas.

We found a place to park, then spent some time wandering through the shops and browsing in an art gallery on the main street. But it was a beautiful sunny day with a light breeze blowing in off the ocean, and we had really come to enjoy the beach.

On the boardwalk an elderly woman sat at a card table, collecting a fee from those who wanted to use the beach.

We paid our money then used the public restroom to change into swimming suits before laying out a blanket and our cooler on the beach, staking out our claim.

As Brianna was sorting through our cooler, I tapped her on the head and yelled, "Last one in the water is a rotten egg!" And then I ran as fast as I could and splashed into the surf before diving into the water. She ran after me but stopped short of the water.

When I came to the surface, I was in pain because the water was so cold. "Come on in! The water's fine!" I gasped. The truth is, I'd lost all feeling in my legs.

"It's not cold?" she asked.

"Oh, gosh, no, not a bit!"

She dipped her toe in the water, then shook her head. "It's too cold for me."

"Hey, it's not bad once you get used to it!" To make my point, I ducked completely under and then came up with a big frozen grin on my face. "See, it's not even cold!"

"If that's true, how come there's nobody else in the water?"

"They were all in the water just before we came, but now they're resting."

"You know what? I think I'll just go back and work on my tan. You can swim if you want, though."

She turned and went back to where our blanket and towels were.

Once out of the water, I had to take a little walk along the beach to warm up because I didn't want Brianna to see me shivering.

When I returned to the blanket, she was lying on her back working on her tan. When I sat down beside her, she sat up and folded her arms across her chest. She was obviously a little self-conscious about wearing just a swimming suit, though it was one-piece and not low cut like most girls were wearing. Even so, I felt uneasy looking at her. After all, Brianna and I had met while serving as missionaries. So this was a pretty big jump.

"How was your swim?" she asked.

"Great. You should try it!"

"Nice try, Adam."

"What are you talking about?"

"The water's really cold, isn't it? You were just trying to con me into getting wet, weren't you?"

"Absolutely not. You think I'd deliberately try to trick you?"

"That's what I think, all right."

We were sitting next to each other, loving the teasing and being teased.

Before eating our lunch we decided to take a walk on the beach. Neither of us had worked on our tans that summer. With the exception of my arms and face, I was almost ghostly white. Brianna wasn't much better. We were both afraid of getting burned so we each put on a T-shirt.

With the waves rolling in, the warm sun, and the light breeze, it was perfect. We had fun following the retreating waves as they flowed back into the ocean, then racing to avoid getting wet as a new wave would break onto the sand. We ended up walking a long way, enjoying the sounds and smells of the sea and stopping once in a while to examine broken shells or skip smooth rocks on the water. On the way back to our spot, I reached for Brianna's hand and she gave it to me. That was nice.

We saw some children playing catch with a big, plastic ball. We stopped and watched. Just for fun, I began to give a play-by-play sports radio description of the game. "Look at that. That is the best catch I've seen all day!" I shouted in my radio voice. The kids loved it that an adult would make a big deal out of their game.

On our way back to our home on the beach, that is, our blanket and towels and cooler, Brianna said, "That was nice what you did for those kids."

"I think it's what my first mom would have done. I keep wanting to be more like her."

"You're plenty amazing already," Brianna said. "You don't need to change."

"How can you say that?"

"Because it's true."

"The truth is, I don't know what I want to do with my life," I admitted.

"You'll find out, and when you do, it'll be good. You're not likely to waste your life on things that don't matter."

As we walked, we talked about everything–things from our childhood and high-school years we'd never told anyone else about.

"I love being here with you," I said. "I've got an idea. Let's just stay forever. We'll sleep in the car at night and spend our days at the beach. Because I'm such a good guy, I'll give you the backseat so you won't have to contend with the steering wheel."

"And where will we take showers?"

"We'll use the public changing rooms. I happen to like the showers in the men's dressing room. I'm sure the women's are just as nice."

"That's a little more public than I'd prefer."

"We'll go early in the morning then."

"I can see you've got this all worked out," she said with a silly grin.

"Absolutely."

"And how will we make enough money to live?" she asked.

"My mom was an artist, so maybe I can become one too. I'll sell my paintings to people who come here every day."

"When's the last time you did any artwork?"

Since I didn't want her to know I'd recently worked on sketching her face, I avoided the question. "Well, let me just say that in the ninth grade, I was very good."

"You mean compared to other ninth graders, right?"

"Some people have natural talent," I said.

"Well, maybe you're right."

"And even if I'm not very good, we'll sell badly done paintings to people without much artistic sense. And in the winter we'll move to Florida."

"What about Thomas?"

"If he can paint a halfway decent beach scene, he can come with us."

"The three of us, then?"

"That's right. The three of us. It's the three of us most of the time anyway, isn't it?"

"Sometimes it is."

We arrived back at our cooler and got out our lunch. Before we started eating, Brianna said, "We should say a blessing."

People were walking by, and I felt a little self-conscious praying like that in public, but Brianna was waiting for me to take the lead.

"You're right. I'll say it," I said.

I gave a short prayer, then we unwrapped our sandwiches.

"Do you think about him when you're with me?" I asked.

"About Thomas? I do, but not the way you think."

"How do you think about him?"

156

"Mostly I compare him with you."

"And your conclusions?" I asked.

"I'm always very happy when I'm with you."

"Too bad I don't have an education, isn't it?"

"You wouldn't be more fun if you had an education."

"No, but I'd be more marriageable."

"You'll get an education at the Y, then those girls will be standing in line for you."

"Right . . . those girls at the Y. That's where my future lies."

We ate in silence for a time, then Brianna said, "Let's just have fun today, Adam. Let's not think about the future."

"I've been doing that very well this summer. I've had so much fun working for my grandfather. I'm not all that sure I even want to go to the Y. I think I'd be perfectly happy just staying here."

"But you've got to get an education, don't you?"

"I don't know." I paused. "Sometimes I think my second mom in Utah has programmed me to follow in my dad's footsteps: marry some girl she's picked out for me; take over my dad's business; and live close to home so my mom will be able to spoil my kids."

"And what would be so terrible about such a plan, if it exists?"

"I don't know. You're right. I'm being too critical of her. But I just can't see majoring in information systems anymore."

"Fine. What do you want to major in?"

"I don't know." I paused. "I want to be . . . more of a free spirit."

She shook her head and laughed. "I'm not sure you can major in that."

"This is all new to me. Is there any problem with a guy taking a little time to decide what he wants to do for the rest of his life?"

"No problem at all . . . as long as it doesn't take him twenty years to make the decision."

157

We broke out some drinks, and Brianna opened a bag of chips. Sitting next to her on the blanket, watching the waves rolling in, and enjoying the food and the sunshine made it an absolutely perfect day. It was true, I would have been happy to stay there all summer.

Brianna must have felt the same way. "This has been such a great day," she said. "Thank you, Adam."

"I'm not bad for a summer fill-in, am I? Of course I know you're just counting the days until Thomas gets the official seal of approval by passing the bar exam. And then you two can get married and spend the rest of your life litigating together."

She gave me an irritated glance. "Here's a little advice I learned from law school. Don't voice opinions on topics you're totally ignorant about."

"Well, thank you very much. I'll write that down when I get home. I'm sure it will be useful. I mean, after all, I've never been to law school."

It was a mean thing to say, and Brianna looked as though she might cry and turned away from me.

"You had to ruin it, didn't you?" she asked.

"Ruin what?"

"Our day at the beach."

"I was just facing reality, that's all. I'm going to move away, and you're going to get married to Thomas. After a few weeks, we'll never see each other again. This was a great day, but it's only one day, and it's not a lifetime."

"I wish it could be."

"Me too. More than you'll ever know. But, you know what, we're not going there, okay?"

I started to gather up our things and preparing to leave. "Can't we stay here a little longer?" she asked.

"No. Our day at the beach is over, Brianna. Let's just go home."

A few minutes later we had packed up, changed back into

our regular clothes, and were on the road again. We didn't speak for the first few minutes.

Finally she broke the silence. "Do you actually think that the only reason I'm thinking of marrying Thomas is because he'll have a law degree?"

"Maybe it's not the only reason, but it is one of the reasons, isn't it?"

She shrugged. "I don't know."

"It's okay. It's natural you'd want someone you can talk to. I mean, someone who speaks your language."

She nodded. "Maybe so."

"If you and I were together, and you started talking about *Roe v. Wade,* I'd think you were talking about a tennis match."

She didn't want to, but that made her smile.

When we pulled in front of her apartment, she said, "Do you want to come in?"

"Is that such a good idea?"

"Probably not."

"I'll walk you to your door."

We got out of the car, and I carried Brianna's cooler to the entry of her apartment. She turned to me. "You know what? Even when we're not getting along, you're more fun than any other guy I've ever known."

"Thanks, I think." I set the cooler down.

"We're friends, so it's okay if you give me a hug," she said.

I took her in my arms and held her.

"We won't kiss, though, right?" I asked.

"Right. That wouldn't be right for us to kiss."

We were hugging with the most innocent of intentions when she looked up at me, and then we kissed for the first time.

We could hear the phone in her apartment, ringing through the door. She stayed in my arms.

"Aren't you going to get that?" I asked.

159

"No."

"Why aren't you going to answer it?"

"It's Thomas. I told him to call me at nine."

"If you don't answer it, he'll be worried."

"If I answer it and get rid of him right away, as fast as I can, will you stay?"

I looked at my watch. "I can't stay here much longer, whether you answer it or not."

"Adam, we really need to talk."

"It's about the kissing, isn't it? Let me guess, this is the *I just want to be friends* talk, isn't it?"

"What do you want, Adam? For us to kiss every time we're together from now on and never talk about what it means? Is that what you want?"

"I don't know what I want. This is really getting complicated."

"I know. We need to talk."

"I'm not ready to talk to you yet, Counselor. I have to prepare my case."

She slammed the door on her way in.

We both knew what we needed. We needed to just be friends. The only problem was that, for me, it was getting more and more difficult to do that.

10

This was the day I was to accompany Brianna when she sang for her stake council meeting. I woke up at five-thirty and couldn't go back to sleep. I lay in bed and stared at the clock, watching as each minute was first proudly displayed by my digital clock and then quietly discarded.

I had never been so conscious of time as I was now, knowing that each day brought Brianna and me closer to the time when our summer would end and we would take our separate paths—me to Utah and she, eventually, to Michigan to begin married life with Thomas.

The thought of saying good-bye to Brianna was depressing enough, but on top of that I dreaded coming to the end of my happy life working for my grandfather. Every day of work was like when a boy wakes up on his birthday and finds a brand-new bike in the living room. I loved fixing people's leaky faucets. I loved mowing lawns, perched on a new riding mower, and then, afterwards, playing Clumsy Monster with the kids who lived there, with their moms watching me make

161

a fool of myself, but, afterwards, thanking me for paying attention to their kids.

I loved living with my grandparents and learning more and more about my first mom. I discovered that in many ways, I was a lot like her. When I would sometimes feel bad because I couldn't seem to measure up to my second mom's expectations, I would remind myself that it was okay—I was just being Charly's boy, Adam.

Dreading leaving Brianna was not my only concern. I got a sick feeling in my stomach when I thought about starting college. Now that I'd ruled out majoring in information systems, I didn't have any idea what to choose. I dreaded the idea of being confined to a classroom, having to study all the time, being bored out of my mind by the dry professors, and struggling to stay awake in the library.

I also worried about what my folks would say when they realized how much I'd changed during the summer. I didn't feel like the same person who'd left Utah in June.

Strangely enough, the one thing I didn't worry about anymore was the temptation to access Internet pornography. Maybe it was the closeness I felt to my real mom or the love I felt from my grandparents or the time I had been able to spend with Brianna, but the idea of watching that stuff no longer tempted me.

My alarm went off at six. I showered and then got ready for church.

At seven-fifteen I entered the Relief Society room in Newark where I would accompany Brianna as she sang "Lord, I Would Follow Thee" for a stake council meeting.

She was sitting at the piano. She stood up to greet me.

"Good morning," she said. She seemed a little standoffish to me.

It's because we kissed last night, and she feels guilty about it, I thought.

"Good morning," I said, trying out the role of distant

162

friend. "Well, we'd better get started. Do you need to warm up?" I sat down next to her on the piano bench.

"I already did. I think we can just go ahead and start."

We practiced for ten minutes, until people began gathering in the room, then we took our seats on the front row.

The meeting began at seven-thirty. After the opening song and prayer, the stake president introduced Brianna. Before she began she thanked me for being her accompanist.

It turned out all right. After we finished, we were warmly thanked and then excused.

We walked out to the parking lot together.

"My grandparents would like you to have dinner with us after church today," I said.

"I'd better not," she said softly.

"I don't agree. I think you should."

"Why?"

"My grandparents love you. Don't punish them just because I tried to kiss you last night."

"It wasn't just a try, Adam. And it wasn't just you. We actually kissed, and it was as much my fault as it was yours."

"So you feel guilty about it?"

"Of course I feel guilty."

"Why? You're not engaged."

"No, but that's just a formality. Don't you think I owe a certain loyalty to the guy I'm planning on marrying?"

"You're right. What happened last night was all my fault," I said.

"No, it wasn't—that's the problem. I don't know what's happening to me. I've always been able to set a course in life and move toward it. And now, I don't know, I can't seem to focus on what I need to do."

"I really hate to see you feeling guilty. Look, I can do better. Let's just be friends while I'm here. I'll be leaving the twenty-first of August. It'll be here before we know it. Let's just keep seeing each other until I go."

"We'll have to be very careful."

"We will. I promise."

She sighed. "All right, we'll try and see how it goes."

"Thank you."

Brianna's block meeting let out the same time as my grandparents' ward, but she had farther to drive, so we beat her to the house. She showed up a half hour later. Once again, she and I were assigned to make a salad, but this time there was no water fight. We were working on decorum that day.

Brianna and I offered to do the dishes. At first Grandma Claire protested, but we told her we were fine and that she and Eddie could just relax. He finally convinced her to let us clean up, and they went upstairs to their room.

After doing the dishes and putting things away, Brianna and I sat across from each other at the kitchen table and read the scriptures. When we came to a passage we especially liked, we would read it out loud and then talk about it.

It was a great feeling to be reading the scriptures with Brianna. It felt safe and comfortable, being together in that way. But it made me also think about how quickly the summer was going.

I said to her, "I woke up early this morning, and couldn't sleep, thinking about how little time we have left."

"It's over a month."

"That's true."

"When I woke up this morning, I felt so guilty about what we did last night. Did you?"

"Not really," I said.

"Have you ever felt guilty for something you did wrong?" she asked.

"Well, yeah. That's what Mormons do—feel guilty."

She laughed but then asked, "So what did you do about it?"

"I went to my bishop and talked to him."

"What did he say?"

"He worked with me. And now it's taken care of."

Her eyebrows raised at the word *now,* but she didn't say anything.

"That's what happened to me," she said. "It was in high school. But even though it's taken care of, once in a while, I still feel guilty."

"No need to."

"You're right."

I paused. "We're not going to tell each other what it was, are we?" I asked.

"No, we're not."

"Good. I really don't care what yours was."

"Me either."

After that we shared scriptures that deal with repentance and forgiveness.

And then we talked about the Savior.

We both felt the Spirit.

It felt good.

So good.

"Thomas and I never talk about things like this. He never seems to have the time to just talk. He's always going a mile-a-minute."

"He'll slow down once he's passed his bar exam."

She put her elbows on the table and rested her chin in her hands. She sighed and said, "I don't think he'll ever slow down."

"You just have to tell him what you want."

"Maybe so." She closed her scriptures and stood up. "I need to go. Thomas said he'd call me later today so I'd better be there."

She headed for the door. "Don't bother to see me to my car. I'll call you tomorrow. Maybe we can work out at the club again."

"That'd be great. I've missed Chanteille."

When my grandparents got up from their nap, they felt badly that Brianna had left.

"Well, maybe it's just as well," my grandmother said. "We need to talk."

"We think you need to tell Brianna how you feel about her," my grandfather said.

"How do I feel about her?"

"You're madly in love with her," my grandfather said.

"I am? Thanks for telling me."

"You are, and you need to tell her."

"What for? She's practically engaged."

"Maybe she'd have second thoughts if she knew how you feel," my grandmother said.

"There's that restaurant with the cliff divers," my grandfather said. "They put on a real good show. Why don't you take her there?"

"She might like that," my grandmother said.

And so, against my better judgment, on Friday, I took Brianna to the Mexican restaurant my grandparents had recommended. The restaurant was three-stories high, with tables situated on little balconies where customers could get a good view of the divers.

I had carefully worked out what I was going to say, even writing it out beforehand and practicing it in front of a mirror. But I pictured a quiet table, where I would softly say, "Brianna, I can't tell you how much I've enjoyed the time we've spent together. My grandparents love you, and I've grown to care about you a great deal as well. If things don't work out between you and Thomas, please remember that I'm here for you." And then I would reach out, hold her hand, and give her a rose.

But once we arrived at the restaurant, the reality of the situation was much different than I had imagined. Our table was next to a waterfall that was so noisy, we could barely hear each other. What with the noise of the falling water and the

166

music blaring during each show, it was hard to even carry on a conversation. In addition, someone in a fake monkey suit was perched on an artificial rock ledge just a few feet from where we were sitting, and the monkey kept staring at us.

After one of the shows, and before we'd been served our food, I saw my chance.

"Brianna, there's something I need to tell you!" I yelled above the noise of the waterfall and background music.

"What?"

"The reason I brought you to this restaurant is—"

"What?"

"Restaurant!"

"Restrooms?" she yelled. "I have no idea where they are, either! But if I have many more glasses of lemonade, I'm going to need one pretty soon too!"

I leaned closer. "I can't tell you how much I've enjoyed the time we've spent together!"

The monkey jumped down from his perch and started toward us.

I stood up and faced him. "Get out of here!" I shouted.

The monkey stood and waved its arms at me.

"You stupid monkey! Go away!"

The monkey shrugged his shoulders and left to go harass some other diners.

I sat down again. "I'm sorry that I had to yell at the monkey in front of you!"

"It's not a real monkey!"

"What?" I hollered.

"It's not a real monkey!"

"I know that!"

"I didn't know if you did or not!" she yelled back.

A guy about my age, wearing red slacks and a pink flowery shirt approached us. "Hello, folks, how's it going? Hey, guess what? I'm the Balloon Man! Would you like me to make a balloon hat for each of you?"

"No, go away," I complained. "And tell everyone else to quit bothering us."

"What about you, pretty lady? Have you seen any of the balloon hats I've made for some of our guests?"

"No, I haven't, actually."

"Well, come, let me show you."

Brianna went to the ledge with Balloon Man. In pointing out hats he'd made for others, he put his hand around her waist and drew her in closer to him.

"We don't want any stupid hats!" I shouted at him.

"I'd like one like that," Brianna said.

He kissed her on the hand. "My pleasure, Señorita."

A few minutes later she was wearing the most ridiculous hat I'd ever seen. I couldn't look at her without wanting to laugh. An orange balloon encircled her head, and there was a green balloon flower stem coming out of the top of her head, and a red balloon fake flower that bobbed on the stem whenever she moved her head.

The good thing was that after the Balloon Man made the hat, he went away. There was also a momentary lull in the diving and the loud music that went along with it. Stupid hat or not, this was my chance. It was the quietest it had been since we got there.

I spit out the words as fast as I could. "I can't tell you how much I've enjoyed the time we've spent together. My grandparents love you, and I've grown to care a great deal about you, too."

"What did you say?"

The announcer's voice suddenly drowned out all other noise. "Ladies and gentlemen, boys and girls, good evening! And now for the best diving show in New Jersey!"

I stood up and walked to the ledge. "Turn down the volume! It's so loud in here I can't hear myself think!" I shouted.

Apparently the divers did not appreciate me complaining.

The first diver dove close enough so that the splash from his dive drenched me.

The monkey made the mistake of laughing. I went over and shook his little monkey shoulders. "I want to talk to the manager."

"I *am* the manager."

"You're a monkey, for crying out loud! How can you be the manager?"

"Okay, okay, I'm not the manager! But he's my uncle."

"Whatever. Look, I need it quiet so I can—"

"Ask your girlfriend to marry you?" the monkey asked, his voice sounding hollow inside his fake monkey head.

"Something like that."

"I can make an engagement hat for both of you!" Balloon Man said.

"Get out of here and leave us alone!"

Balloon Man looked very disappointed, and the monkey looked, well, like a monkey. But they did leave.

I sat next to Brianna while she watched the diving show. As soon as it was over, I leaned close to her so she'd be able to hear me. Even so, I had to speak real loud. "Brianna, there's something I need to tell you," I fairly shouted.

As she turned to face me, her extended balloon flower bopped me in the nose.

She started to giggle. "Sorry!"

Just then two waiters brought us our food. Just my luck—hers was on fire.

"That's it, I give up!" I complained. I hunched over my food and ate it as fast as I could. I just wanted to be out of the place.

"You okay?" Brianna asked.

"Great, just great," I muttered, with my mouth full of food.

"There's something I need to tell you, Adam," she said, raising her voice.

"Is it something serious?" I yelled.

"Yes."

"Then take off that stupid balloon hat."

She removed the hat. "Thomas called me last night!" she shouted.

"What'd he say?"

"He told me he thought I was spending way too much time with you!"

I figured she was about to tell me she couldn't see me anymore. So, wanting to take her home as quickly as possible, I took another huge bite of food.

She looked at me in shock. "I can't believe you can get so much food in your mouth in one bite."

With my cheeks bulging, I could only scowl at her.

"Do you want to know what I told him?"

I meant to say, "Sure, why not?" but I'm sure she couldn't understand a word I said.

"I broke up with Thomas last night!" she said.

"Huh?"

"I realized I don't love him enough to marry him. Adam, I know you're going back to Utah, so this is really bad timing, but the truth is, I really think I'm in love with you. It just sort of snuck up on me. One moment we were friends, and then, all of a sudden, bam, there it was."

Shredded meat is very hard to chew up in a hurry. Especially half a pound of it. It seemed to take forever.

"Take your time. We're in no hurry," she said.

Finally I finished. "I was going to tell you the same thing."

She got a silly grin on her face. "You broke up with Thomas, too?" she yelled.

"No, not that part. The part about being in love."

"So that means that you and I—" she began.

The monkey was back.

Brianna stood up and waved her hands. "Get out of here, you stupid monkey!"

The monkey scurried away.

"Thank you," I said, mouthing the words so she could read my lips.

"No problem." She reached for my hand and leaned close to my ear. "I'm not sure what just happened here."

"You mean with the monkey?" I asked.

"No, not the monkey. I mean the part about us being in love."

"I know. That's new ground for both of us, isn't it?" I said.

"It is, for sure."

"What are we talking about here?" I asked, sorry I had to say it so loudly.

"I don't know. I haven't dared think that far ahead."

Unfortunately the monkey was onto us. "Engagement Time!" he shrieked.

Waiters came running toward us and put Mayan head-pieces on us and joined in a happy engagement chant. And then they shook our hands and took our pictures and brought us a free dessert.

Five minutes later, another show began.

"Let's make a run for it while we can!" Brianna shouted at me.

We barely managed to escape.

I drove Brianna to her apartment, where we sat on the front steps and talked until we were both too tired to say another word. I walked her to her door, we kissed a couple of times and then she pushed me away. "Now that we're in new territory, I'm booting you out of here," she said.

Notwithstanding the disaster at the restaurant, I drove home a very happy guy.

11

That same night, as soon as I got home, I went to my grandparents' room and knocked. "Grandmother? Grandfather? I need to talk to you both. It's very important."

My grandmother came to the door and opened it. "Is something wrong?"

"No. Everything's great! Brianna broke up with Thomas! She told me she thinks she's in love with me!"

"Oh, that is such good news!" she turned on the ceiling light. "Eddie, wake up! Brianna broke up with Thomas!"

He sat up in bed and rubbed his eyes. "She what?"

"She broke up with Thomas! Isn't that great?"

"It's an answer to prayer, that's what it is! This calls for a celebration!"

They put on their robes, and we went down to the kitchen and had hot chocolate and Graham Crackers. They insisted I tell them every detail, which I was happy to do.

We laughed and ate and talked until past midnight, and

then we had family prayer, gave each other a big hug, and went to bed.

After getting ready for bed, I went into my room and to my closet and retrieved my mom's paintings as well as my sketches of Brianna. As I looked at each one, I tried to imagine what my first mom's reaction would have been if she'd been alive to get to know Brianna. I was sure she'd love Brianna and be very happy for me.

At that one instant in time I felt so alive and happy and content with my life. Everything was going so well for me now. I had a better idea of who I was. And I was in love. And I would probably be getting married sometime soon. How could anything be better than that?

I sat at the harp and plucked a few strings. For some reason it seemed to anchor me to my first mom. I don't know why, since she quit playing it soon after her folks bought it.

Even though I didn't remember her, I felt a real connection to my first mom and wished I could talk to her. I remembered the story my dad had told me of when she knew she was dying and pleaded with me not only to say Mommy but to remember her.

Now it was me wondering if she remembered or thought about me, or if she was too busy in Paradise to think about her son.

"Mom, please remember me because I love you now."

I glanced out the window. The sky was beginning to turn gray. I wanted to spend as much time as possible with Brianna on Saturday and needed to get some sleep. And so I slipped between the sheets and soon fell asleep.

I slept until noon. When I finally got up, I found a note from my grandparents, telling me they'd gone to get groceries.

I shaved, showered, grabbed something to eat, and called Brianna on her cell phone. When she answered, she told me she was at work and that she wouldn't be home until six.

"Since when do you work Saturdays?" I asked.

"My boss called me at eight-thirty this morning. They have an important case that needs immediate attention. And guess what? He's putting me in charge of the whole thing. That means no more making other people look good. I'm my own boss on this! Isn't that exciting?"

"Yeah, sure, great! Good for you!"

"Thanks."

At six o'clock I was sitting in my car in the shade of a tree in front of her apartment when she pulled into the parking lot.

We hurried toward each other and hugged.

"That's what I've needed all day!" she said as we walked hand in hand to her apartment.

"Me too. I was going crazy waiting for you. I was so desperate I was about to commit a crime just so I could have you for my lawyer."

She laughed. "I'd have defended you for free. My day has been awful too."

"What happened?"

"Well, it's fairly complicated . . . and boring, actually."

I couldn't help wondering if she thought I would never be able to understand what she did every day at work. But I didn't let it bother me.

She let us in and then headed to her room. "I'll be right back. I need to change. You're welcome to anything in the fridge you can find."

She came back in a few minutes, barefoot and wearing a pair of khaki pants and a T-shirt. She opened the refrigerator. "Have you eaten?"

"Not yet. You want to go out?"

"No, let's do with what's here." She grabbed a carton of eggs and a green pepper, some cheese and a package of sliced ham from the refrigerator, then began to cut the green pepper into tiny pieces.

I came up behind her and wrapped my arms around her waist and kissed her on the back of her neck.

"That feels nice."

"I love you," I said.

"I love you too, but I missed lunch and so, right now, I am starving! So let me work, okay?"

"How about if I go read your paper?"

"Sure, that'd be good. Oh, one thing, it's the *Wall Street Journal.*"

"Yeah, so?"

"Well, it's not the most exciting reading you'll ever find."

"Is that it, or is it that you don't think I could understand it?"

She laughed. "Adam, I don't know anybody who completely understands the *Wall Street Journal.* But, you go ahead and try if you want. Then explain it to me."

I read a couple of articles in the paper but couldn't understand them. I started turning pages. "They got any comics in this paper?"

She laughed. "That's what I asked the first time I read one."

We sat and ate and talked. And then, all of a sudden, it hit me. "This is so great!"

"You like the omelet that much?"

"No, not that. It's you and me, sitting around the table, eating a meal together, talking about our day. I mean, think about it, we could be doing this, day after day, for the rest of our lives. It makes me really happy to think about us together."

She leaned over and kissed me on the cheek. "It makes me happy too."

I went into the living room and brought back the *Wall Street Journal.*

"A little light reading, hey?" Brianna said.

"Something like that." I looked at the article I had read. "What does it mean to buy a hedge fund?"

She laughed. "Leave it to a gardener to come up with that question. What do you think it means?"

"People who invest in hedges?"

"Sounds good to me."

I set aside the paper. "I'm serious."

"About what a hedge fund is?"

"No. I want you to teach me everything you know, so when you come home you can tell me what happened at work and I'll be able to understand."

She nodded. "All right. We can do that. It might take a little while though."

"Let's get started."

"Really, right now? I've had a killer of a day, Adam. Can't we just talk? How did your day go?"

I told her about the party my grandparents and I had the night before, after I told them she'd broken up with Thomas.

There was a loud knock at the door.

She got up from the table. "That's my boss," she said. "He told me he might bring over some papers for me to look at before work on Monday."

She opened the door and gasped. I looked up and saw Thomas, but he hadn't yet seen me.

"Thomas, what are you doing here?" she asked.

"I need to talk to you. Can I come in?" He didn't wait for an answer. Once inside, he saw me at the kitchen table. "Have you moved in here already?" he asked me.

"No, just visiting."

He turned to Brianna. "We need to talk. Alone."

Brianna looked shocked but said, "Let's go outside. Adam, will you excuse us?"

They ended up just outside the front door. Because Thomas had trial lawyer's voice, I could hear what they were saying.

"Don't tell me you're actually considering marrying that . . . that custodian, or handyman, or whatever he is."

"It's definitely a possibility."

"What is wrong with you anyway? Why would you do such a stupid thing?"

"He makes me happy."

"Tell me the truth, Brianna. Are you pregnant? Is that why you're thinking of marrying him?"

"I can't believe you said that."

"What is it, then? I mean, good grief, use your head. He has no education. You'll end up supporting him. And how much do you two have in common? And what do you two talk about? Why throw away your education for someone like him? Okay, he has a good tan, I'll give him that, and a fair build, but, come on, are you really that shallow?"

"It's true he doesn't have an education, but he's not stupid. He can learn. I mean, just tonight, he asked me to help him understand the *Wall Street Journal.*"

"What word did he have the most trouble with? *Wall* or *Street?*"

At that point, I'd had it. I opened the screen door and stepped outside. "I think you'd better go now."

"If you really care about Brianna, don't marry her."

"Why?"

"Because you'll never be able to appreciate her like I do."

"You mean because of my lack of education?"

"It's not your lack of education. You could always get an education. No, the thing you don't know is that she's brilliant. I'm afraid you'll turn her into some overweight, frumpy, soccer mom with twenty kids, too tired all the time to make any kind of contribution to society." He turned to me. "What year in college are you?"

"I'll be starting this fall."

"As a freshman?"

"Yes."

"Have you picked a major?"

I paused.

"Oh, sorry, am I going too fast for you? If I am, you just let me know and I'll slow down. Do you even know what it means to choose a major in college? Or does the word *college* have you stumped?"

"Thomas," Brianna cautioned.

"You haven't picked a major yet, have you?" he asked me.

"I was going to major in information systems, but—"

"Let me guess. You changed your mind. Look, no hurry. Take all the time you want to get through college. Five, ten years, it's all good."

"Thomas, you'd better go," Brianna said.

"Does Lawnmower Man here know how much your student loans are?"

"No, we haven't discussed that yet."

"I think you'd better. He might have second thoughts about getting into a marriage with someone who has student loans well over one hundred thousand dollars!"

My mouth dropped open.

"Surprised? Shocked?" Thomas asked. "It's typical for students who go to Columbia Law School. The reason people are willing to get into that kind of debt is they generally start at high enough salaries they can pay off their loans in a few years." He turned to Brianna. "Does he know how much you're earning now?"

"No."

"Maybe you should tell him," Thomas said.

"Why should I do that?"

"It will give him something to shoot for."

"He doesn't have to make that kind of money."

"No, but who is going to make payments on your student loans while he's going to college? The Tooth Fairy? Santa Claus? Or maybe he can get a few more lawn mowing jobs? I hardly think that will cover it, Brianna."

178

He poked his finger at me. "I don't have anything against you personally, but I do strongly object to the mess you're both going to get into if you get married. You have no goals, she's goal driven. You like mowing lawns. She likes pitting her intellect against the best legal minds in the country. If you're happy, she'll be miserable. If she's happy, you'll feel like a failure."

He turned to Brianna. "That's why I got in my car and drove all the way here. It's not just because I don't want to lose you, Brianna. It's not just because I thought you and I would make a good team. No, it was much more than that. As your friend and as your colleague, I beg you both to reconsider a marriage that will bring you nothing but grief. Okay, I know money and debt and earning power aren't that romantic, but they are facts of life, and they do break up marriages.

"You two may be attracted to each other, but that's not going to pay the bills. I admit I tend to look at cold, hard facts, but in a case like this, that's not such a bad idea."

I wanted to rip this guy's head off, but I knew I couldn't do that.

The one thing I didn't want to do was argue with him. And so the only thing I could think of was to poke fun at him. I started clapping. "Great job! I'd give you a solid A. Look, if you ever need a letter of recommendation about courtroom technique, you just let me know."

"Have you got anything to say for yourself?" he demanded.

"Yeah, I do. I'm in love with this girl. And she loves me. That's all that matters."

"If you think that, you're living in a world that doesn't exist," Thomas said. "I'm going now, Brianna, but this isn't over. I love you too much to give up without a fight."

After he left, we went back into the apartment and sat down at the kitchen table for a long time without saying anything.

"How much are your student loans?" I asked.

"One hundred and twenty thousand dollars."

"How much do you make?"

"Seventy thousand a year, but it should go up in a few months."

"Oh. What will it be then?"

"I don't know. Maybe ninety thousand a year."

I felt awful. "That's real good."

She nodded.

We were just a few feet apart from each other, but it seemed like a mile.

"If we got married and moved to Utah to go to BYU, could you get a job there as a lawyer?"

"Eventually. I'm not licensed to practice law in Utah. But I could get some kind of a job there."

"It wouldn't pay as much money, though, would it?"

"No, probably not."

"Well, then, I'll just change my plans. I won't go to BYU."

"But that's what you've always wanted to do, isn't it?"

"I don't care about it now. You're more important to me than anything else."

"But you need an education."

"Why?"

"Because I don't want to work when we have a family."

I stood up. "I need to go home and try to figure out what we're going to do."

She came to me and we held each other in our arms.

But somehow, it wasn't the same.

12

For the next couple of weeks, Brianna and I didn't see much of each other. She worked late every night. We saw each other for maybe an hour after she got off work.

"Why are you working so hard?" I asked one Sunday after church.

"They're trusting me with something that is very important. I just don't want to let them down."

"When will you be done?"

"In another week or two."

"We need to talk about our plans."

"I know. We will, just let me get through this first."

Another week dragged by with very little contact between us.

On the first Sunday in August, I went with her to church. After church she spent the afternoon with my grandparents and me.

We didn't talk about what our plans were. I think we were both afraid to bring up the subject, worried it would somehow

181

cause us to break up. Instead, after we ate and helped clean up, we sat at the piano and sang hymns together.

While we were still sitting next to each other at the piano, she told me she'd be in Washington, D.C., most of the week. "I'll be giving a presentation at a Senate sub-committee hearing. It's a big step for me."

"Good for you."

"Sorry. I wish I could get out of it. I'd rather spend my time with you. But maybe it won't be too bad. We can e-mail each other all week."

"I don't do e-mail."

"What are you talking about? Everybody does e-mails."

"I don't."

"Why not?"

"I'd rather not say. We can talk on the phone."

She shook her head. "I'll be very difficult to get hold of."

"Just call me when you get back to your room."

"It might be late."

"It doesn't matter. Call me anytime."

She had a puzzled expression on her face. "Okay, but . . ."

"What?"

"Nothing."

She didn't phone until Thursday night and that was at two in the morning to give me details of her return flight and ask me to pick her up at the airport.

She'd awakened me out of a sound sleep, but I managed to write down the time, 6:35, that her flight would get in the next day. And then, almost immediately, I fell asleep again.

At four-thirty Friday afternoon, I had just finished mowing the lawn and was playing Clumsy Monster with some children from one of the apartments.

My cell phone rang and I answered it, still chasing the kids.

It was Brianna. "How's the traffic?" she asked. "I know it's a Friday and things are probably backed up."

"What?"

"You are coming to get me, aren't you?"

"Yeah, sure. It's too early to leave now. You don't get in until 6:35."

"I get in at 5:36 P.M."

"I must have written it down wrong."

"What are you doing now?"

"I just finished mowing the lawn."

The kids started squealing as I chased after them.

"You're playing with children again, aren't you?"

"Well, just for a minute. Like I said, I just got done mowing the lawn."

"Adam, we're about to board my flight," she said, biting off each word. "I am totally exhausted. I don't want to wait around for you at the airport. Look, just forget it, okay? I'll take a cab to my place."

"I'll come right away."

"I told you when my flight was coming in. I thought I could depend on you to come get me."

"Maybe you told me the wrong time."

"No, Adam, I did not tell you the wrong time."

"I'm in my pickup right now. Here I come, ready or not."

"I'll wait ten minutes for you. If you're not there, I'll take a cab."

The traffic was heavy. I was still miles away from the airport when she called me from a cab and told me to forget about coming to get her.

"I'll meet you at your place," I said.

"That's not going to work. I'm exhausted. All I want is to take a shower and go to bed. I'll see you tomorrow."

"Okay."

"I've had such a rotten week. And to think I have to go back there on Monday."

"You were gone all week. I thought you'd be done."

"I did too, but these things are complicated and take time."

"Did you talk to Thomas this week?" I asked.

There was a long pause. "We traded e-mails a few times during the week. But it was mostly professional. I needed to run something by him. He's really quite competent, you know." She paused. "Oh, and he called me this morning."

"Of course. After all, you are colleagues. Look, if you're ever in one of these hearings and you need some information about the best way to mow a lawn, feel free to call me."

"I'm too tired for this, Adam."

"Sorry. I'm giving a talk in my grandparents' ward tomorrow. Do you want to come and hear me?"

"I've been asked to fill in and play the piano in Primary for someone. But I could come over afterward."

"Come hungry then."

"All right."

When we said good-bye, I felt depressed and helpless. *Thomas is poisoning her mind against me, and there's nothing I can do about it.*

On Sunday afternoon, when she showed up at my grandparents' place after church, we couldn't connect with each other. She was still in her lawyer mode and seemed distant.

My grandparents carried the conversation by asking many questions about what she'd done at the Senate subcommittee hearings.

"Sounds like you did a great job!" my grandfather said. "I'm surprised they didn't offer you a job on the Supreme Court."

"Oh, believe me, I have no ambitions to do that."

"Well, you're smart enough, that's for sure. We're so proud of you!" my grandfather said.

After we ate, Brianna and I sat in the living room, facing each other, grim-faced and silent.

"We're not very talkative today, are we?" I said.

"Sorry, it's just that I'm so tired. I can't believe I have to do this all over again tomorrow ."

"Everybody has things they have to do over and over again. Take me, for instance. I have to mow the lawn each week, but do you hear me complaining?"

She raised her eyebrows and shook her head.

"What?" I asked.

"Nothing."

"No, go ahead, tell me what you're thinking."

"Must you compare every situation in life to mowing lawns? Are you trying to be some backwoods dispenser of folk wisdom, or do you do it just to make me mad?"

"It just comes naturally. You see, compared to you, I am dumb."

She stood up. "I can't talk to you when you're like this."

She was on her way out when I called out her name.

She stopped and turned to face me.

I walked over and put my arms around her. She sighed, drew closer to me, and rested her head on my shoulder.

"I love you," I whispered.

She let out a huge sigh. "I know. Me too. I'm sorry for being such a witch today. I got so hammered this past week. And then I kept thinking about what Thomas said. About us. He has a point, you know. When we're married, how are we going to get you through college, pay off my stupid student loans, and have children all at the same time?"

"I'll figure it out by the time you come back next week. I'll have a plan, and everything will work out. You'll see."

She nodded. "I hope so."

She kissed me on the cheek then told me she had to go home and get ready for Monday and then get some sleep.

She was gone until Wednesday, just one week before I'd told my folks I would be leaving for Utah. But none of that mattered because I had a plan.

185

I picked Brianna up at the airport. It had been raining all day, and her flight was forty-five minutes late.

I drove her to my grandparents' place. We ate a late dinner. For the first time in many days, I was upbeat and positive. I asked my grandparents to be with us while I unveiled my carefully thought-out plan.

"Okay, I've got everything figured out," I said enthusiastically. "And I've got a little something here for you, Brianna!" I waved a small box containing an engagement ring. "So, ladies and gentlemen, sit back, relax, and enjoy the flight!"

I wanted my grandparents in on the plan too.

"Okay, here we go. Here's my plan! I'll stay and work here. Brianna, you keep working where you're at so you can make good progress in paying off your school loans. We'll get married in a few months. It's perfect, right?"

"Well, it's an interesting plan," she said diplomatically. "So, will you go to school somewhere around here?"

"No, I'll just keep working. We'll pay off your school loans faster that way."

"So, you're not going to go to college?"

"I might sometime, just not right away."

She chose her words carefully. "So, in your plan, do I keep working my whole life? Because, once I have kids, I'm not going to want to work."

"You can quit once we pay off your student loans."

"And what will you be doing, if you don't have a college education?"

"Lots of people don't have college educations."

"Yes, but most of them have a skill or a trade."

"I'll figure something out." I looked at my grandfather. "I haven't talked to you yet, but maybe when you retire I could take over managing the apartments."

"The man who owns them lives in England. He's told me he's going to sell them in a year or two," my grandfather said.

"I thought you owned the apartments."

"I owned one of them at one time, but I sold it, and got hired to manage the three buildings. I'm just a hired hand. Once the buildings are sold, we'll both be looking for work. Well, except I'll just retire then."

I began to panic. "I'll find another job."

"Why don't you work for your dad?" Brianna asked.

"I don't like to do that kind of work anymore."

"But you're good at it, and it pays well," Brianna said. "Your mom told me."

"It's not . . . who I am now. I'm not like that."

"What do you mean, you're not like that?" my grandmother said. "Good grief, it's just a job. What difference does it make what you do as long as you bring in money? If you're good at something, do it."

"No, I can't do that anymore."

Grandmother said, "What do you mean, you can't do it anymore? You've forgotten how? I don't believe that for a minute."

Everyone was looking at me. I started to stammer. "See, the thing is, I'm more like my first mom. You told me that she used to say, 'Life is for fun.' Well, creating Web sites is not fun. So I don't want to do it. I don't want to be like I was."

My grandparents looked at Brianna to see what her reaction would be.

"You've taken this too far, Adam," my grandmother said. "You've created an image in your mind of what your mom was like, but it's warped, and it's not the way she really was. She had a 3.7 grade point average in college while she was working twenty hours a week doing commercial art. Yes, she did say life is for fun, but, let me tell you something, she worked her tail off to put herself through college."

My grandfather added, "You're treating Charly like she was some kind of a saint. But she wasn't. She was just like most of us. She had some good qualities and a few bad ones." He paused. "Like with Mark, for example."

187

"Eddie, we are not going to talk about Mark!" my grand-mother snapped.

"Who's Mark?" I asked.

My grandmother pointed a warning finger at my grand-father. "Eddie, not another word! Do you hear me? Not one word!"

"He needs to know that Charly had her problems too."

"Is Mark someone she went with before she met my dad?" I asked.

"You could say that," my grandfather said.

"Don't say another word!" my grandmother said.

"Why not? It was before she even joined the Church!"

That was all I was going to learn about Mark. But it was almost enough. I knew my first mom had gone with him. And I knew they didn't want me to know about their relationship.

I could almost connect the dots. "Did she sleep with him?"

"Eddie, you see what you've done?" my grandmother wailed.

"It was before she joined the Church," my grandfather said.

I felt like I'd just lost my identity. During the summer I'd put so much effort into seeing the similarities between my first mom and me, that I'd come to believe that I was like her in every way. But, at the same time I'd done that, I had also distanced myself from my dad and my second mom, so that now, discovering that my first mom wasn't perfect, I felt like I didn't have anyone I could put my trust in.

Right then I knew I desperately needed some time to think. Time by myself. Like when I'd driven out from Utah. Maybe if I took a little more time going back, it would help me sort things out.

I put my hand to my forehead and just started rambling. "You know what? I think I'll just head back to Utah now. I mean, I was going to leave in a week anyway, but, you know what? I have a lot of things to do to get ready for school in the fall. So I think I'll just pack up and leave now, if that's all right. Yeah, that's what I'm going to do. Thank you very much for a wonderful summer. I've had a good time, and it's really been . . . educational, but I really think I need to go home . . . to my family. Excuse me, I need to get packed up. Oh, Eddie and Claire, would it be all right if I took some of my first mom's things? In case I ever want to look at them again. Which I'm not sure I ever will."

Leaving Eddie and Claire and Brianna, I hurried upstairs to my room and began throwing everything I'd brought with me from Utah in suitcases and boxes and carrying them out to my car.

"Adam, we need to talk," Brianna said at the bottom of the stairs as I passed her with some boxes.

"No, I can't talk to you. You know what? Thomas is right. You'll be better off without me."

I returned to my room and boxed up all my mom's things too. And on my last trip I crammed the harp into the trunk. It stuck out, so I used some string to tie the trunk lid as much as I could over it.

"I'll call and let you know how I'm doing," I told my grandparents on my way out the door for the last time. They looked stunned, and I knew my leaving like that was killing them. But I was too frustrated and confused to think about anything but getting away from there.

Brianna was standing between me and my car. "Tell me what's happening," she said.

"I don't know."

"I love you, Adam."

"I know you do. Me too." I stopped to hold her in my arms. "I'm so messed up, Brianna. I'm sorry." I broke away from her and then hurried to my car and drove off.

I headed west, and it seemed fitting when it began to rain. Soon, it was coming down so hard, the windshield wipers could barely keep up. An hour later, I came over a small hill and saw a stalled car in the road ahead of me. I slammed on my brakes and went into a long, slow spin on the rain-wet road. The string I had used to tie down the trunk snapped, and the harp was thrown out onto the road. Miraculously, I managed to stop before I hit the car, then pulled off to the side of the highway, grateful no one had smashed into me from behind.

As I was getting out of my car to go pull the harp out of the road, a semi-truck came over the hill and ran over it, sending splinters of wood and bits of wire everywhere.

"Nooooo!" I shouted.

13

I spent the night in my car in a vacant lot along a side road, not far from where the harp had fallen out of the trunk. As soon as it got light enough to see, I walked back to the scene of the accident. There was nothing left of the harp except some splinters of wood and some loose wires. I picked up what I could and then returned to my car.

I felt empty and sad, not just because the stupid harp had been destroyed, but more so because, the night before, I'd been so quick to write my mom off just because of learning about one mistake she'd made in her life. I had my own mistakes to deal with. Why was I so judgmental about someone else's? Also, I knew I'd treated Brianna badly too. How could I just drive to Utah and pretend our love for each other had never existed?

I wasn't sure that running off to Utah and abandoning my grandparents and Brianna was the thing to do. It was true I needed time to figure things out, but did I have to be thousands of miles from Brianna to do it? There was only one place close by that came to mind.

I turned the car around and drove to the ocean at Spring Lake. I got there about seven-thirty in the morning. It was a blustery day, and it was threatening to rain. I didn't mind because I just wanted to walk along the beach and think.

I walked for an hour north along the beach and then turned around and headed back.

My feelings were all messed up. I felt like I was lost in a giant maze and couldn't get out.

When I passed the place where I'd parked my car earlier that morning, I saw a woman setting up a card table; she was there to collect two dollars from everyone who came to the beach.

I walked until about ten o'clock in the morning. By that time, I was starving.

Leaving the beach, I walked past the woman at the card table. She was a frail, white-haired, aristocratic-looking woman, and it was hard to imagine she was doing this for food money.

I handed her my two dollars.

She looked at me strangely. "You're leaving and you're paying me?"

"I'll be back."

She smiled. "I had someone tell me that once when I was about your age. He never came back, though."

"How foolish of him."

She smiled. "That's what I thought too."

She took my money and stamped my hand.

"Do you do this every day?" I asked.

"Yes, every day."

"Looking at the way you dress, I'd guess you don't do this for food money."

"No, nothing like that. I do it for civic pride. We want to keep our beach area picked up. That takes money."

"Makes sense."

"You're not from around here, are you?"

"I live in Madison."

"But you're not from there either."

"No. I'm from Utah."

"So you saw the light and had the good sense to move here, is that right?"

"I did. I might go back to Utah though. I can't decide."

"Why go back?"

"I'm supposed to start at BYU fall semester, but I'm not looking forward to it."

"Why's that?"

"I met a girl."

"Oh, of course. There's always a girl."

"I'm really hungry. Is there a good place to eat near here?"

"My sister runs a bed and breakfast. Her name is Julia. Oh, I'm Catherine. Tell her I sent you. She'll take good care of you."

She gave me directions to her sister's bed and breakfast. The place was only two blocks away, in a wood frame, two-story house.

A hand-lettered sign next to the front gate read, "Sea View Bed and Breakfast." Below that sign was a similarly lettered sign that read, "No Solicitors." It seemed a strange combination—welcoming people and turning them away at the same time.

A woman answered my knock. She also had white hair, and it was obvious she was Catherine's sister.

"Yes?"

"Catherine sent me."

"You're too early if you want a room."

"I don't want a room. I just want breakfast."

"This is a bed and breakfast. It's not a breakfast."

"Catherine said you'd take care of me."

The woman made an exaggerated sigh. "She'll be the ruin of me yet. Well, all right, I suppose you can come in."

I stepped inside.

"Take off your shoes and your socks."

"My socks too?"

"You've been walking on the beach already, haven't you? You think I want sand scattered all over my house? No, sir, I don't."

I removed my shoes and socks.

"Come this way. Don't touch anything."

Her house could only be described as a shrine dedicated to figurines—mostly ballerinas.

She had me sit down in the dining room. There were some dirty plates on the table, but whoever had been there for breakfast had left.

"What I'd like is—"

"Did I ask you what you wanted? No, I did not. You come here, you're a guest in my home. I don't ask guests what they want for breakfast. You'll get what I fix you, and you'll eat it all up, or you'll be hearing from me."

"Yes, ma'am."

"I will now go and fix your breakfast. Make yourself at home."

She left. There wasn't a newspaper to read or a TV to watch. But I didn't mind. I had a lot to think about.

Ten minutes later Julia brought in my breakfast. It was more than I'd ever eaten in my life—pancakes, real maple syrup, bacon, two eggs, and cranberry juice.

"This looks great!"

"Eat every bit of it or you're not leaving the table."

I raised my eyebrows. "You get much business here?"

"All I want. I don't need much. Just a little extra to get me by."

It wasn't just because I was so hungry, but it was the best breakfast I had ever eaten.

"That was great! How much do I owe you?"

"Seven dollars."

I pulled out my wallet. "Do you take Master Card?"

"I take cash."

I fumbled through my wallet. "I've never been to a place that didn't take a credit card."

"Well, you have now."

"All I have is four singles," I said.

"You owe me seven dollars."

"I know. I'll need to go get some cash from an ATM."

"We don't have an ATM in town."

"Well, I'm sure there's one somewhere."

"This is a small town and we want to keep it that way. We have no desire to turn Spring Lake into Coney Island. That's why we take pride in not catering to tourists. Believe me, it's no accident we don't have an ATM in town."

"What do the people do who stay here?"

"My regulars know the rules. And when someone makes a reservation, I tell 'em to bring cash. Of course, once in a while, someone walks in with no cash."

"What do they do?"

"They usually promise to mail me the money when they get home."

"I could do that too."

"The problem is not everyone who promises actually sends the money."

"I promise. I'll find a town with an ATM and then come back with the money. I'll be gone at most two hours."

"How do I know you'll do that?"

"What do you want me to do then?" I asked.

"Is there someone you can call and have them bring you the money?"

I thought about Brianna, but I wasn't about to call her and ask for a favor—not after I had left her so abruptly.

"She wouldn't do that," I said.

"Who wouldn't do that?"

"My girlfriend."

"Your girlfriend wouldn't help you out?"

195

"Actually, she's more like my *ex*-girlfriend."

"I don't know what to tell you then."

"We'll figure something out. Can I use your restroom?"

"You'll have to use the one on the second floor. The one on this floor doesn't work."

I smiled. "Today is your lucky day then. I'll fix whatever's wrong for what I owe you. How would that be?"

"Are you a plumber?"

"No, better. I do maintenance on three apartment buildings in Madison that my grandfather manages."

"Well, you can take a look at it if you want. Just don't make it worse than it already is. I called a plumber two days ago, but he hasn't come yet. You know how it is with plumbers."

I looked at her toilet, went to a hardware store, bought less than two dollar's worth of parts, and within another ten minutes, had her toilet working.

"I'm finished. Come and see what I've done."

She entered the room a skeptic, but after flushing a few times I became her newest best friend.

"You are truly a gifted man."

"So is my breakfast paid for?"

"Yes, absolutely." She put her hand on my arm. "I have a few other things that need fixing. If you'll work around here this afternoon, I'll give you dinner."

"Sure, why not?"

I had her show me the things that needed fixing, then went to the hardware store for some materials and parts, and then started in. For the most part they were easy jobs, the kind I did all the time for my grandfather.

I was done by one-thirty.

"I belong to a bridge club," Julia said. "I've been talking to the ladies. They have things that need fixing too. If you're willing, I'll go with you to these ladies' homes, and you can work your magic with them. You work so fast I'm sure you'll be done in no time at all."

I shrugged my shoulders. "Sure, whatever. I don't have anything better to do."

"You're a rare man who is willing to take a few minutes to help someone in need."

Julia rode with me to each place. They were mostly old houses, small, modest, two-story, wood-frame houses, with only two or at most three bedrooms. Most of them had the same plumbing that had been installed when the homes had been built many years earlier.

These women, now widows, were silver-haired, frail women, who didn't have enough money to remodel and couldn't afford to move.

They all said they'd called plumbers but could never get them to come. I thought it was more likely that a plumber would want to do more than these women could afford, and so, after a while, the plumbers just quit responding to their calls.

"If you can't fix it, I'll understand," the first woman said. "Nobody else has been able to. They always want to replace everything. Why should I replace it? This one is perfectly good, if it would only work."

"I can fix it."

"I'm not sure you can, dear, but I would greatly appreciate it if you would try."

Ten minutes later the repair was done.

I went in the kitchen. "I'm finished."

"Oh, well, let's take a look," the woman said, afraid to get her hopes up too high.

"Oh, my! Would you look at that!" she said as she flushed the toilet.

"Isn't he a marvel?" Julia raved, then turned to me. "There's no doubt about it. You, my friend, are the Tolstoy of Toilets, the Picasso of Plumbing, the Rembrandt of Repair."

It felt good that someone thought I was worth something.

"Well, let's go, time's a wasting," Julia said. "We have many more to visit before you get dinner." She laughed. "It's so much fun to have an indentured servant. I think we should bring that practice back, don't you?"

We visited five more of her friends. The houses were old and in need of lots of repairs. I took care of the immediate problems and promised to come back and do more. By four o'clock in the afternoon we were finished and went back to Julia's place. The meal was prolonged because each of the women whose plumbing I had fixed brought a special dessert or hot dish for me. Since I couldn't eat all that food by myself, I invited the ladies to eat with Julia and me. And so they did.

You'd have thought I was a movie star or some kind of celebrity, the way they fussed over me. They were all so complimentary and gracious and had such great stories to tell about when they were my age.

Catherine, Julia's sister, joined us. "Well, Adam, you're quite the ladies' man, aren't you?" she said.

I laughed. "I guess I am."

"Thank you for being so kind to us."

"My pleasure."

"Where are you going after you leave here?" Julia asked.

"I'm not exactly sure."

"I have a small cottage in the back. You're welcome to stay there for free if you'll keep working for my friends and me."

"Actually, I am between . . . jobs."

"Then stay here. We're nice people, aren't we?"

"Very nice."

"Then stay."

So I moved in. I agreed to do the plumbing and home repairs for Julia and her friends almost for free. They would pay for the parts and materials and give me a little extra for gas money and such, but I would essentially be their slave.

The next day I took Catherine's place at her post at the

card table and collected money from everyone who came to the beach. In the afternoon I worked for Catherine and Julia's friends.

That evening, I called my mom and told her I would not be starting at BYU in the fall.

"What are you going to do?"

"I just need to find myself, that's all. I'm fine. I've got a job, and I'm staying with good people. I'm doing mostly repair work on homes. Let me give you my phone number and address in case you need to get hold of me."

I also called my grandfather and told him what I was doing and where I would be staying. He tried to talk me into coming back to work with him, but I told him I couldn't do that. At least, not right then. I asked him to tell Brianna I was okay and that I'd call her sometime.

And then I took the battery out of my cell phone and threw it in the trunk of my car.

I didn't go to church on Sunday. I just didn't feel like it.

A few days later Brianna came to the beach while I was on duty at the card table. I watched as she parked her car and then walked toward me. I panicked. I didn't know what to say, and I couldn't even guess what she was going to say to me.

"That will be two dollars, please," I said.

She handed me a couple of dollar bills.

"I'll need to stamp your hand," I said.

She let me do that.

"Enjoy yourself at the beach."

She didn't move.

"So, how's Thomas?" I asked.

"He came to visit me. In fact, he just left yesterday."

"And did he give you a ring?"

"He *showed* me a ring. I didn't take it, though."

"Holding out for something more expensive, right? That's my girl. Columbia Law School must be so proud of you."

"I don't deserve that kind of treatment, Adam."

I sighed. "You're right. I'm sorry. How about if I treat you like everybody else who comes here? Have a nice day and don't forget to put on sunscreen!"

A couple with two little kids stopped to pay their money. "You're in the way here," I said to Brianna.

She stepped aside so the dad could pay me.

After they left, she asked, "What are your plans?"

"I don't have any."

"Are you going to go back and work for your grandfather?"

"No, probably not."

"Why not?"

"I'm settled in here now. Everybody loves me. I'm a productive citizen of this community. I'm sure that's a shock to you."

"How long are you going to stay here?"

"You're badgering the witness."

"You owe me something, Adam. I need to know what you're going to do."

"What *can* I do? What can *either* of us do? You have to keep working to pay off your loans. That, of course, will take years, even if you keep working for the same law firm. And if I go to college, then that just adds to the time it will take us to pay off our loans. So what *do* we do?"

"I'm sure we can work something out. I'm very disappointed in you, Adam. I don't understand why you'd just walk away from me and your grandparents and just . . . just give up."

I stood and turned to face the beach. The wind had picked up and it began to rain. I shook my head. "My problem isn't that I don't know what to do." I sighed. "My problem is—I don't know who I am."

I risked one painful look at her. "Brianna, until I figure that out, I'm not going to be much use to anyone."

She had a hurt look on her face, but I didn't care about

her pain as much as I did mine. "You know what? You'd be better off marrying Thomas."

She stood there in the rain, looking at me as though I'd slapped her, then turned and hurried away to where her car was parked and drove away.

Other than that, and the brief rain shower that drove all the visitors into the shelter for half an hour, it was a pretty normal day at the beach.

14

I have a vivid memory from when I was very young, maybe four or five, of sitting on the floor with a new set of building blocks on Christmas Day, putting together a fort by stacking one block on top of another. I remember choosing each block carefully and making sure the stacks were straight and neat.

That was how I felt about what I was doing while staying with Julia and Catherine. I was starting from scratch to define who I was and what I was going to be in the future.

What would I adopt into my new life? I could choose anything I wanted because nobody in Spring Lake really knew anything about me. I could become whoever I wanted to become. I had, in some ways at least, severed all connections to family and friends. I was on my own, and everything from the past was on the chopping block.

It turns out I wasn't the first to have stayed in the cottage for an extended period of time. Julia told me about Mr. Appleton. He had stayed there almost a year before one day disappearing, never to be heard from again.

"We've kept all his things in the garage," Catherine said.

"How long has he been gone?"

"Almost two years now," she said.

"I think we should toss his things," Julia said. "We're not a storage dump. We need to be able to use our garage. Will you go through Mr. Appleton's things and throw out everything you think he won't care about if he shows up some day and asks where his things are?"

I started right away. The first thing I did was haul all his boxes from the garage into the cottage. I picked a box and began going through it.

In the first box I found a framed picture of Mr. Appleton. He was of slight build, wore a mustache, combed over his bald spot on top with hair from the sides, and in the picture was wearing a bow tie.

"What kind of man was he?" I asked Julia at lunch.

"He was a quiet man," she said. "He didn't talk to many people and stayed in his room most of the time. Once in a while we'd see him on the beach. He'd always wear a white shirt with his swimming suit. He never went swimming though. Mostly he just sat on a towel and watched everyone else."

I returned to my work. A few minutes later I came across a cardboard box that had been taped shut, whereas the others had just had been closed by interlocking the flaps.

I undid the tape and opened the box and saw that it was filled with pornographic videos.

It was a shock seeing them. My first impulse was to watch them. There was a TV and videotape player in the cottage. I could have locked the doors and viewed them right then or done so late at night.

But then I thought about Mr. Appleton. I looked at his picture again and imagined him in some tiny apartment, all by himself, with the blinds pulled, going through the same pathetic routine, day in, day out, for the rest of his life. And when he died, who would mourn him? Who would care that he lived or died? No children to mourn him. No wife to miss him. No loved ones or friends to talk about his contribution to their lives.

This is not who I am, I thought. *Not now and not ever!*

I carried the box outside, went to the garage, grabbed an ax, returned to the box and smashed every video into pieces. Then I stuffed the remnants into trash bags and dumped the bags into garbage cans that would be picked up in the morning.

As I was chopping them up, I felt a sense of power. It felt good to have faced an old temptation and to have come away victorious.

That was the first characteristic I chose for the new me. I would not become a slave to a terrible addiction.

Saturday night a new challenge arose, and that was whether or not I would go to church in the morning.

The question that came to my mind was: Is the only reason I go to church because of my mom and dad? Did I serve a mission only because I was told that's what I should do? Did I live the Word of Wisdom only because of my family? And, if that is so, then if I separate myself from my family, do I end my involvement in the Church?

The answer should have been obvious, but in my state of mind, it wasn't clear to me.

Julia asked me what I would be doing on Sunday. I said I didn't know.

"You could come to church with us."

"Why do you go to church?"

"Because we believe in God. Don't you?"

I had to think about it. "I guess I do."

"Then you should go to church."

It seemed like a good argument, so I changed my mind and decided to go to church. By going to the library and checking phone directories, I found that the nearest ward was in North Brunswick. I called and learned from a recorded message when the meetings were held.

And so I went to church. People there seemed happy to see me. A counselor in the bishopric asked me how long I'd be in the ward. "I'm not sure. Maybe for a long time."

"We could use your help," he said.

"Thanks. I'm glad somebody can."

The next week, I again tried to reconstruct myself from scratch. In a way it was an exciting experience, deciding what would be the foundation of my life and what I could discard.

I began praying and reading the scriptures again. Not because I was supposed to, not because I'd been told to do it, but because I needed the comfort I'd always found in prayer and scripture reading.

After two weeks I had pretty much fixed everything that Julia and her friends had for me. But by then word had gotten around about a new fix-it man in town.

I began to charge for the work I did. Not much at first though. I was just glad to be considered useful.

Julia would only let me work for someone she approved. She said she was worried about people who might take advantage of my willingness to help. But Julia also had a higher criterion. There had to be an overriding reason, other than saving money, why I would work for someone.

One day, just as we were about to eat dinner, the phone rang. Julia picked it up. "Yes, he's here, why do you ask?"

She listened. "All right, I'll ask him if he'd like to help you." Julia turned to me. "This is a couple who teach school in town. They've got a leaking pipe. They just got home, and there's an inch of water in the bathroom, and they can't stop it."

"Get their address. I'll go right over," I said.

Their names were Derek and Elizabeth Conroy, and they were standing at the front door of their house waiting for me.

I immediately liked them. In spite of the emergency, they

were able to joke about it as they escorted me into the bathroom. The bathroom floor was covered with water, and there was a dark patch of soaked carpet several feet into the hall.

They were an energetic couple in their early thirties. Derek was nearly bald and had a beard. He wore slacks and a turtleneck. Elizabeth had short hair, and a pixie face. With her energy and enthusiasm, she reminded me of someone who'd play Peter Pan onstage.

I checked the pipes under the sink, but they weren't leaking. I turned off the water to the bathroom. "Do you have a mop? Let's get rid of the water on the floor first."

"What do you think caused this?" Derek asked.

"I'll tell you in a minute," I said.

"Are you hungry?" Elizabeth asked. "We're having shish kebabs. I can put one on for you."

"No, thanks. I'm fine."

"I'm putting one on for you anyway."

I suspected the wax seal at the bottom of the toilet had cracked and begun to leak. With the water turned off at its source, I flushed the toilet to empty the bowl and tank, then loosened the mounts and lifted the toilet off its base and set it off to one side on the bathroom floor.

"Are you a certified plumber?" Derek asked.

"No. But I do this all the time."

"I'm sure you do, but I can't really figure out what you're doing, moving the toilet."

"Derek, quit harassing the nice man and come and eat!" Elizabeth called from the kitchen.

"She's right, sir," I said. "Don't worry. I know what I'm doing."

"Well, all right." Reluctantly, he went and joined his wife.

"He called you, sir, didn't he?" Elizabeth teased. "You're getting to be so grown-up!"

I loved the way she laughed.

I discovered I'd been right. The wax seal was cracked in

206

two. On my way to my car, I said, "I've found your problem. I'm going to the hardware store for parts. I'll have you back in business in no time."

"Great!" Elizabeth said. "I'm not above going next door and asking to use their bathroom, but my husband is a bit old-fashioned. I've seen that pained look on his face before. For his sake, I hope it won't take too long."

"I don't have a pained look on my face," he said.

"You do, Derek, you definitely do. Next thing, you'll be jumping up and down."

Thirty minutes later I had replaced the wax seal and had the toilet working again. I charged them for parts and then asked an additional twenty dollars.

"Is that all you want?" Derek asked.

"Yeah, that's all."

"Stay for your shish kebab," Elizabeth said. "It's your reward for fixing us up so fast."

"Well, that's very kind of you, but I really should be going."

She thrust the shish kebab toward me like a sword. "Look, I don't want to hear another word from you! Take the kabob and sit down and eat! Derek, you're excused to use the bathroom."

Derek hesitated.

"This nice man won't think less of you if you excuse yourself. You can even turn on the fan so we won't suspect what you're doing." She turned to me and winked. "We won't know, will we?"

Derek nodded and went to use the bathroom.

"Sit down and start eating," she said. "I've got dessert too. Baklava from a Greek restaurant. We get it take-out once a week."

We both sat down.

"Catherine says you both teach in town," I said.

"We teach at the middle school. He teaches science, and I teach English."

"How do you like doing that?"

"We love it. The thing is, we can make a difference in these kids' lives. We can change the world one kid at a time. That's what's so exciting about it."

We heard the fan go on.

Elizabeth laughed. "My husband is so predictable, but I love him dearly."

"I can see that."

A few minutes later Derek rejoined us.

It was comfortable being around them. They were so animated and happy and excited about life and their work as teachers.

I ended up staying another hour. We ate and talked. Mainly I asked them about teaching. They were all too happy to tell me.

"You seem awfully interested in teaching. How come?" Elizabeth asked.

"I'm not sure I'm interested in teaching. It's just that I want to make a difference. I want to wake up in the morning excited about what I'm going to be doing. I want to believe that I'm doing something to make the world a better place."

"That's teaching!" Elizabeth enthused.

"Or plumbing," Derek said. "You certainly made our world a better place."

"Of course some days as a teacher are the worst days of your life," Elizabeth said. "But on other days, it's exciting to see a student who's been struggling suddenly catch fire. On days like that, there's no better feeling."

All the way back to my cottage, I kept thinking about what it would be like to be a teacher—to make a difference in a boy or girl's life. It sounded great to me.

Spring Lake has two kinds of people, those who live in elaborate homes and those who don't. For the most part, I dealt with those who didn't have much money. Word got around, and I kept busy.

But in the second week of September, Julia got a call from one of the richest women in town, a woman in her late seventies by the name of Mary Livingston Cartwright.

"I hear you have someone staying with you who can fix things," Mrs. Cartwright said.

"He has been known to fix things, but I'm not sure he'd want to work for you."

"I hate trying to get people to come. They say they'll be here on a certain day, but they don't show up. So you call them and they make another promise and they show up four hours late. And then they tear everything apart and don't show up again for weeks. Please, let him come and work for me."

"Well, let me talk to him. Please hold the line."

Apparently, Julia and Mrs. Cartwright had previously had some run-in, and Julia couldn't help tainting the request. "You want to do work for someone who's rich and snooty?"

"Why did she call me?"

"She can't get good help."

"I'll do it."

"She won't pay you what you're worth."

"Nobody else has."

"She never talks to Catherine when she comes to the beach. Oh, no, she's too good to talk to the help."

"Even rich people have plumbing problems."

Julia shrugged. "All right, go fix her problem, I don't care one way or the other."

I laughed. "I can see you don't care."

Mary Livingston Cartwright lived on the street that

fronted and ran parallel to the beach. The house was a four-story mansion built in 1947 by a weapons manufacturer who made a fortune during World War II.

Mary Livingston, the daughter of a minister, had married into the Cartwright family. Together she and her husband had raised three children who had long ago left the state. Her husband had been dead for fifteen years, and she was now seventy-two years old and lived alone in that big house.

I had to ring four times before she came to the door. She looked like she was dressed for a party that should have been held forty years before. She wore a long pink dress with feathers sewn around the collar. I was fairly certain nobody made dresses like that anymore.

"I'm the plumber. You talked to Julia about me."

She shook her head. "Go away. I've changed my mind."

"Did someone come and fix your problem?"

"No, nobody came."

"Then why would you change your mind?"

"I don't want a stranger in my house. You never know these days. Now go away before I call the police." She started to close the door.

"Would you like me to come back with Julia or Catherine?"

"I don't know them either."

"Catherine is the woman who collects money from people who use the beach. You've probably seen her sitting at her card table. She's there every morning."

"I don't have ticket takers for friends."

"She doesn't get paid for it. She's a volunteer. You must have seen her if you've ever gone to the beach."

Mrs. Cartwright hesitated. "Perhaps if you bring her, I will let you in."

It took a long time to make the arrangements. First I had to talk Julia into working at the beach for an hour, and then I had to convince Catherine to go with me.

Finally we showed up on Mary's doorstep and were allowed inside.

Catherine and Mary sat in the parlor and carried on polite conversation while I worked in the four bathrooms in the house.

I had to make three trips to the hardware store.

"How much is this going to cost?" Mary asked.

"I won't be able to tell you until I'm done."

"I'm not a rich person," she said.

It looked to me as though Mary was being held hostage by faucets that leaked and toilets that didn't always flush. It must have been years since she'd had anyone in the house to fix the problems.

I worked for two hours before I was finally done.

By this time Mary and Catherine were at the kitchen table, eating fancy sandwiches with no crusts and filled with a cream cheese-green olive mixture they'd made together.

"I'm done."

"It certainly took you long enough. Did I mention I'm not a rich person?"

"You did. Would you like to see what I've done?"

"Yes, I would. I just hope you haven't made things worse."

"Oh, don't you worry about that," Catherine said. "Adam here is very good."

It took her a while to climb to the fourth floor, and then we worked our way down. I pointed out everything I'd fixed.

By the time we reached the bottom, Mary Livingston Cartwright was very grateful. "Oh, thank you, thank you for doing so much."

"No problem. I spent twenty-seven dollars and forty-nine cents at the hardware store."

"So how much do I owe you?"

"Forty dollars."

"Is that all?"

"Yes, Ma'am."

"Well, you've got to let me do something for you. You've spent all this time working and you've done so much. There must be something I can do."

I walked into the kitchen to make sure I hadn't left any tools lying around. "Does that finger sandwich have cream cheese in it? I'd be pleased to have it."

"I can make more," she said.

"No, just that little corner piece would be plenty for me."

"Please take it then."

I popped it in my mouth.

She walked us to the door. She and Catherine gave each other a little hug.

Mary Livingston Cartwright turned to me. "Young man, in all my days, I've never heard of someone coming to make repairs who didn't charge an arm and a leg."

"I'm just happy to help out."

"Let me put you on retainer."

"What does that mean?"

"It would be like an insurance policy. I would pay a certain fee every month with the understanding that if I need you to fix something, it won't cost me anything, except for parts, and that you will promise to come within two hours of when I call you."

"I'd do that anyway, without a monthly fee."

"Please let me talk to my lawyer about it. I'm sure we can work something out, not only for me, but for all the houses on this street."

"Well, it's not necessary. Just keep your fridge stocked with cream cheese and green olives. That's good enough for me."

"What is your name?" she asked as we were leaving.

"Adam Roberts, ma'am."

"Adam Roberts, you are the finest young man I have ever known. Your folks must be so proud of you."

I shook my head. "No, actually they're not. They're very

212

disappointed in me, but that's a topic for another day. Good-bye, Mrs. Cartwright."

On the way out to the car, Catherine took my arm. "You hate cream cheese and green olive finger sandwiches, don't you?"

I nodded. "But don't tell anyone, okay?"

"Oh, Adam, my sweet boy, you have captured the hearts of everyone in this community."

"That's kind of you to say."

"Where is this girl who once loved you?"

"I don't know. She's probably married by now."

"What is her name?"

"Brianna Doneau was her maiden name. She was engaged to a guy named Thomas Marler."

"And she's a lawyer who works in Newark. Is that right?"

"Probably not anymore. She's probably married and moved with her husband to Michigan, where they will both practice law. He has a bright future ahead of him. That's why it never would have worked out between us."

"It's a crying shame she can't see what you've become."

I shrugged my shoulders. "What I've become is nothing special."

"No, you're wrong. Your parents would be proud of you."

"I guess we'll never know, will we?" I said.

I should have known that Catherine never asked questions just to pass the time of day.

♦   ♦   ♦

We endured torrential rains every day during the last week of September so that by Friday night, I had cabin fever and needed to take a walk along the beach. The forecast for the rest of the weekend was not promising. A hurricane was skirting parallel to the coastline and there was a possibility it

213

might turn west and head inland. But nobody could say when and where that might happen.

At eight-thirty I put on a yellow rain slicker with a hood and walked briskly to the beach area. It was already dark, and there was nobody else around. I headed north. The surf was up and waves were crashing onto the beach. It would rain steadily for a while, and then there would be a sudden deluge that would last a minute or two, and then it would go back to being steady again.

I walked for an hour and then turned around and headed back.

When I was about half a mile from the Spring Lake beach shelter, I saw a dark figure approaching me. As it got closer, I could see the person was also wearing a yellow slicker. I was surprised anyone else would be out on a night like this.

We seemed to be on a collision course. I didn't want to talk to anyone, so I changed my direction slightly.

The stranger changed direction also, so he or she was still heading toward me.

I stopped and turned to look out at the waves, hoping the walker would go on by me without the necessity of us talking.

I soon became aware that the stranger in the yellow slicker was standing next to me.

"Got a match?" she said.

I turned and saw that it was Brianna. My first impulse was to escape.

"What do you need a match for?"

"I don't need a match, but that's what you're supposed to say when you meet on a beach on a dark night."

"What are you doing here?"

"We came to talk to you."

I looked around. The beach was still empty. "We? You got a clam in your pocket?"

"Come with me and see. They're in the van."

"You must be married if you have a van, right?"

214

"Hold my hand and I'll take you there."

"I know where that's from. *West Side Story*."

She grabbed my hand and led me to the street where a long van was parked with the engine running.

"Get in!" she yelled.

"Are you working for the Mafia now?"

"Get in, I said!"

I opened the side door. In the few moments the dome light was on, I caught a glimpse of my second mom, sitting in the passenger seat and my dad behind the wheel. "Sit down and move over so I can get in!" Brianna instructed.

I got in and scooted over, and Brianna sat down beside me and closed the sliding door.

"What's going on?" I asked.

"We've all come to see you," Lara said.

I turned and looked behind me. My grandparents on my dad's side were in the seat directly behind us. And in the last rows were my grandparents on my second mom's side, as well as Eddie and Claire.

"We're all here," Claire said.

I was stunned. "What for?"

"We need to talk," Lara said.

My dad drove us to Julia and Catherine's house. I didn't have to give directions. They seemed to know where it was.

The ten of us entered the cottage where I was living. There weren't enough chairs, so I went to the garage, got six more, and set them up in the tiny living room.

As we were sitting down, I looked around at the unexpected scene. All my relatives, except my brother, Quentin, were there. Along with Brianna. I felt like I was having an out-of-body experience.

Once we were all seated, my dad took charge. "We have a few things we need to talk about as a family."

"If this is about trying to talk me into moving back to Utah—"

"It's not about that," my dad said.

"What is it about then?"

"It's about us being a family," Lara said.

"We're going to start clear back at the beginning," my dad said. He sounded in charge, but then he looked over at Lara, who nodded, as if she were giving him permission to continue.

"Adam, I loved your mom very much," my dad said. "She often turned my very predictable world upside down, but I loved her." He sighed. "More than I can say."

The wind and the rain were getting worse, and the bare branches of a tree were beating on the window.

"We'd had trouble getting pregnant, so when you came along, we were very happy. Life was so good for us for a while, and then your mom got sick. As she got worse, it was a very hard time for me." He cleared his throat. "And when she died, a part of me died with her."

Lara reached over and held his hand.

"I had a pretty rough time of it for a while, and then I met Lara, and she helped me so much." He sighed. "Looking back on it now, maybe I should have waited before getting married again. The reason I say that is because I was still grieving Charly's death, and it wasn't fair to Lara. Some days I was like the walking dead.

"Even after a year I wasn't in very good shape," my dad said. "But, you know what, you can't call a time-out in life. You were growing up, and you needed a mom.

"Lara knew that, so I'm sure because of that, she agreed to marry me."

Lara interrupted him. "That's not entirely true, Sam. I loved you. I loved you both. I couldn't imagine my life without either of you."

Dad leaned over and kissed Lara on the cheek. "This woman is my hero, and I will always be grateful for her rescuing me, and for being such a wonderful mom to you."

216

There was a knock on the door and then Julia and Catherine came in with a basketful of sandwiches and some soft drinks. "I bet you people are starving. Eat these up. Let us know when you need more."

"You didn't need to go to so much trouble," Lara said.

"Nonsense. We'll get out of here now and let you talk." And with that, they left.

"Let's finish this up and then we'll eat," my dad said. He cleared his throat. "Adam, there's one thing you need to understand from tonight. It was Lara who rescued both you and me. She was the strong one those first few years."

Grandma Whyte spoke up. "Lara used to call me in tears about how hard it was for her, with Sam still grieving, about to lose his business, and, even at times, Adam, how he ignored your needs."

Lara shook her head. "I'm not Mother Teresa. I just did what needed to be done."

"In time I did get better," my dad said. "But by then, we were in a pattern where Lara took charge of most everything in the family. I should have been more of a leader, but, the truth is, I wasn't. I'm sorry about that now."

Lara turned to Eddie and Claire. "I apologize for not including you more in Adam's life. I was young and insecure, and there were times when I was very jealous of Charly, and I think that jealousy caused me to not be as friendly as I should have been."

"We know you were going through a hard time," Claire said.

"As long as we're clearing the air here, you need to know how hard it was for us," Eddie said. "Adam was our first and only grandchild. We wanted to be involved in his life. But the way things went, we didn't even feel comfortable sending him presents. I still have the toy train set I bought for him, except for the caboose, which I let Adam take with him to Utah."

My dad's mom, Grandma Roberts, spoke up. "Eddie and

Claire, we should have been more sensitive to that need and made a stronger effort to keep you involved. I'm so sorry. It was bad enough to lose your daughter, but to have lost touch with Adam must have made it even worse."

Grandpa Roberts nodded his agreement. "I apologize, Eddie. We had always been so close, as business associates. It seems a shame to have lost contact over the years. Especially since we share a grandson."

"I think it's time we put the entire train together, on the same track," Lara said.

"We're a family," my dad said. "Everyone here is in our family. And Quentin on his mission is also in our family. And the thing is, we need to look out for each other. If one of us is having a tough time of it, then the rest of us need to pitch in and help out. That's what families do."

My mom looked at me. "Adam, what are you thinking?"

"I can't believe you all came here to see me. I didn't think anyone cared about me, one way or the other."

"How could you think that?" my mom asked.

"Somehow I got the idea growing up that as long as I did what you wanted me to do, then I was acceptable to you, but if I ever stepped out of line and did anything you didn't approve of, then you'd write me off and forget all about me."

"We love you no matter what you do," she assured me.

"And what do *you* think about this crazy mixed-up family?" Claire asked Brianna.

"I love your family." She was struggling to keep from getting too emotional. "I don't have one of my own anymore."

"What do you mean, you don't have a family? Everyone has a family," Grandmother Whyte said.

"My dad left us when I was in high school, and then a few years ago, my mom died."

"Be in our family then," Eddie said.

"I'd love to be included in your family."

"All in favor say 'aye,'" Eddie said.

Everyone said "aye," except for me.

"Then it's settled. Brianna is an official member of our family."

My mom glanced at me and winked, "I wonder how we could make it even more official," she said with a silly grin on her face.

"Yes, I wonder that, too," my dad said.

"Are we about done here?" Grandpa Whyte asked. "The only reason I mention it is that I'm starving. They fed us on the plane, but I'm not sure what it was. Whatever it was, there wasn't enough there to fill up an ant."

"Wait," I said. "Don't you want to know what my plans are for how I'm going to make a living?"

"What kind of sandwiches are they?" Grandfather Whyte asked. "I just hope they're not egg salad. I can take anything but egg salad."

"How are you going to make a living?" my dad asked.

"I'm going to be a plumber and repairman for Spring Lake. And if that doesn't work out, I may go to college and become a teacher."

Eddie was out of his seat checking out the sandwiches. "This one is ham . . . This one is ham . . . This one is cheese . . . Oh, here's a tuna. Anyone want tuna?"

"Be whatever you want to be," my mom said. "We don't care, as long as you're happy."

That was as long as she could keep the men in my family from rushing the food. She turned to my dad and said softly, "We'll need a blessing on the food."

My dad asked Eddie to say the blessing.

After the blessing, we attacked the food. Within a couple of minutes, my mom and my grandmothers went next door to help Julia and Catherine prepare some more food.

Half an hour later, Julia rushed in to tell us the hurricane was headed inland. We turned the TV on and watched the Weather Channel.

We were just outside of the area where they expected the hurricane to come ashore, but we were in an area where they were forecasting high winds and heavy rain.

Julia invited us all into her house, and then she started assigning rooms where people could spend the night.

I turned to Brianna. "You can sleep in the cottage. I'll sleep in here on the couch."

She nodded. "Thanks."

"No problem."

"If you two were married, you could both sleep in the same room," Eddie teased.

"What do you think?" I asked Brianna.

She looked a little worried. "About what?"

"About us getting married?"

"This better not be your idea of a proposal," my mom warned.

I was worried that this family-orchestrated proposal might end up scaring poor Brianna off.

"It's late," I said. "Brianna, come with me and help me change the sheets."

She nodded. "Good night, everyone. I love you all!"

"We love you too!"

In the cottage, Brianna and I pulled the bedding off my bed and made it up again with clean sheets. We tried to be efficient and robotic about what we were doing.

While she was putting on pillow slips, I started for the door. "I'll see you in the morning. If you get flooded out, or anything, come into the house."

"Thanks. Good night, Adam."

"Good night." I paused. "Brianna, I've never stopped loving you."

"Me, either. Good night, Adam."

What with the wind gusting to seventy miles an hour and the rain periodically coming in sheets, it was nearly impossible to sleep. And, of course, knowing that Brianna was sleeping in my bed, even though I wasn't there with her, didn't help, either.

By seven-thirty the next morning, the worst of the storm had passed. It was still raining, but with nowhere near the intensity it had during the night.

The phone started ringing. I wanted to sleep, so I didn't get up to answer it, but I could hear Julia in the kitchen pick it up, take a message, and then hang up. No sooner did she hang up than it rang again.

Finally, at eight o'clock she came into the living room where I was sleeping.

"Wake up, Adam. You've got pretty much the whole town wanting you to come and do some repair work on their places."

I got dressed, then went into the kitchen to look at the list of people who had called. Alongside each name, Julia had written down the damage they needed to get fixed.

I sat down and began to work out where I needed to go first. Water lapping at the foundation of a house took preference over a screen door ripped off its hinges.

My dad came downstairs, found out what I was doing, and then went to wake up my three grandfathers.

Brianna wandered in, saw what was going on, and offered to help.

Half an hour later, the men in our family, Brianna, Lara, Grandmother Whyte, and Claire left to go battle the elements. Julia and Catherine volunteered to cook for us, and Grandmother Roberts agreed to work the phones.

I went to each house, introduced either my grandfather or my dad, and then moved on to the next place.

Finally, Brianna and I were dropped off by Grandmother Whyte at the home of Mary Livingston Cartwright. Her house, being next to the beach, had been severely pummeled by the storm.

There were two inches of water on the first floor and water

damage on the second floor where the branch of a tree had broken a bedroom window, allowing rain to pour into the room.

The electricity was still out, so there was no possibility of using a wet-dry vac, which I didn't have anyway. We called Grandmother Whyte and asked her to go to the rental place and rent one. We'd use it once the electricity came on.

The only thing we could do was start mopping up. Brianna and I started in the living room. We worked as hard as we could because we wanted to save the hardwood floors and expensive antique furnishings.

Mrs. Cartwright, in her trademark feathered evening dress, watched us work. "Oh, thank you, thank you. I'm so glad you could come right away."

It took us three hours before we were done. We called Grandmother Whyte. She came and got us.

"How are we doing?" I asked.

"We're keeping up. People keep asking how much they owe you. We haven't known what to say."

"Twenty dollars, plus materials."

"You'll never get rich that way."

"No, but I'll have a lot of friends."

We worked most of the day.

The last place we visited was the apartment of Derek and Elizabeth, the dynamic school-teaching duo.

"Oh, my gosh! It's Plumbing Guy, Derek, and he brought his wife with him. Let's fix 'em shish kebabs," Elizabeth said.

"We don't have any electricity!" he called out.

"He rains on my every parade," Elizabeth joked. "Please, come in. And you must be Mrs. Plumber Guy."

"I'm Brianna. We're not married," she explained.

"Well, you'd better get it done soon, kiddo. The last time your boyfriend was here I flirted with him shamelessly, and I even gave him my best shish kebab."

"That was your best one?" I teased her.

222

"Derek, you've got to come in here. Plumber Guy just said something funny. And he brought his . . ." She looked at us. " . . . plumber's assistant."

"Friend," I said.

"His friend. And she's a girl."

Derek came in. He'd been trying to roll up the carpet that had been soaked by the rain, but it had proven too hard for just one person.

"Can we help?" I asked.

"Yeah, that'd be great."

We rolled up the carpet, lugged it out to the garage, and draped it to dry over the bed of an old pickup Derek was in the process of restoring.

A short while later Brianna and I met all the others at Julia's place.

Everyone had a story to tell about their day. It was exciting for us to have all worked together as a family to help people get through an ordeal.

By this time the electricity had come back on, which was good, since Julia and Catherine had been making pizzas all day, and so now, with the oven working, we sat around and ate and talked and waited for the next pizza to be done.

Our meal took two hours, and by that time the rain had stopped and the storm had passed completely over. It was early evening.

"You want to walk along the beach and see what the storm did?" I asked Brianna.

"That'd be great."

The storm had created a new beach, and it was awesome to see what the winds and rain had done.

It was Brianna's idea to reach for my hand as we walked.

"I have decided to stay in Spring Lake and be a fix-up guy."

"You're already that."

"I'll start charging more now."

"Good idea."

"That's what I'm going to do. What are you going to do?"

She cleared her throat. "My plans are a little up in the air right now."

"Can I ask you a question?"

"Sure."

"What about Thomas?"

"It's over between us—for good."

"How come?"

She thought about it. "We were too much alike. It would be like marrying myself. I don't want someone who thinks exactly like me."

"I'm not much like you."

"That's true." She got a wicked smile on her face. "But, you know what, to tell you the truth, I'm not sure I even need you. I'm already a part of your family. So what would I gain by marrying you?"

"I'll make you laugh."

"You make me laugh already."

"I'll keep your feet warm at night."

"I have naturally warm feet."

"I'll give you children."

"Oh, you will, will you? You're just going to walk up and give me children? Really? Where will you get 'em from?"

"The Kid Store."

She laughed. "So that's how it works! I've always wanted to know."

We continued walking. "So, really, Adam, what have you got to offer me?"

"I love you more than anyone could ever love you."

She nodded. "I love you the same way."

"So have we reached an agreement, Counselor?"

"I'll expect a proposal."

"In writing?"

"No. Just get down on your knees and propose."

"The ground's wet."

"Poor baby."

I knelt down on the sand, held her hand, and said, "Brianna, I love you. Will you marry me?"

"Of course I will, you silly boy."

She pulled me to my feet and we embraced and kissed.

◆　◆　◆

Brianna and I were married in the Washington D.C. Temple on Tuesday, March 18. It was as close as we could get to the one-year anniversary of Eddie and Claire's baptisms. We were there with them when they went through the temple for their own endowments, then joined our family in the sealing room where first they were sealed together as a couple and then Brianna and I were married.

Brianna and I and my mom spent a few minutes together in the celestial room of the temple following the sealing, after everyone else had gone to change into street clothes.

"Do you have something you'd like to tell me?" I asked my mom.

She nodded. "It's just a thought I had in the session. Let's see. How can I put this into words?" She pursed her lips. "When you were a little boy, you tried so hard to be a good boy and to please me. I taught you to put away your toys, and you did that every night, just because you knew it would make me happy. That's the kind of a boy you were."

"Hard to believe that now, isn't it?"

She smiled. "What I want to tell you today is not about keeping things in their proper place."

"Okay."

"Last summer you learned a great deal about your first mom. From that I think you wanted to please her, to be the kind of person she'd want you to be. Is that accurate?"

I thought about it for a moment. "Yes, it is."

225

"And then with Brianna in the picture, there was one more woman to try to please. Did it get tough, trying to please three women?"

I glanced at Brianna and smiled. "It did, actually."

"This is what I learned from being in the temple today. Adam, choose any career in life you want, as long as it's honorable work. Be the best home repairman in New Jersey, if that's what you want. Or the best teacher if that's the path you choose. You don't have to please me. You don't have to please your first mom. Just please Heavenly Father, and you'll do all right."

She gave me a hug and kissed me on the cheek. "You're not my little boy anymore, Adam. You're a man, and you're in charge." She hugged me again, then hugged Brianna. "I'll leave you two alone."

She turned to leave the celestial room. "Mom?" I called out after her.

She turned to face me. "Yes?"

I took both her hands in mine. "Thank you for always being there for me. I'm very grateful to you for being my mom. I love you more than I can say."

"Thank you, Adam. You can't know how happy that makes me feel." She then left the room.

Brianna and I stayed a few more minutes, sitting on a couch together, holding hands and just enjoying the beauty of the room and our own private thoughts.

Finally, we got up to leave. One of the temple workers, a sweet, frail little lady with white hair, who had been assigned to be in the celestial room, stopped us. She took my hand. "Excuse me, was that your mother who left a few minutes ago?"

"Yes."

"Who were the other two women who came and sat down with you on the sofa?"

"There was nobody sitting with us," Brianna said.

"No, there were. I saw them."

I stopped to think about it. "Was one of them young?"

"Yes. Just a few years older than you, I would guess."

"Was she beautiful?" I asked.

"Yes, very. She seemed very happy to be there with you both."

"Is she here now?" I asked.

"No, both of them left a few minutes ago."

"The other woman, what was she like?" Brianna asked.

"She was maybe in her early forties and had long, dark hair. She paid particular attention to you."

Brianna and I turned to each other. Tears were streaming down her face. "Our moms were here, weren't they?" she asked.

"They were," I said.

She wiped at the tears with a tissue. "I'm so happy."

"Me too."

We held hands and walked out of the room, happy at the special gift given to us on our wedding day.

◆　　◆　　◆

Magazines sometimes run articles with the title, "What Women Really Want from a Man."

I know the answer to that question. A woman wants a man who listens to the Spirit and who strives to do what Heavenly Father wants him to do. I know it won't be easy, but that's the task that lies ahead of me.

A woman also wants a man who knows who he is.

Finally, I know who I am.

I am Adam, the son of my father, Sam, and my birth mother, Charly, raised by a loving mother, Lara, married to righteous, wonderful Brianna.

I am Adam and now, finally, I am on my way.